*helio*graphica

UNCONDITIONAL LOVE

Pet Tales by the Humans who Love Them

Compiled by

Avie Townsend

*helio*graphica

UNCONDITIONAL LOVE
Pet Tales by the Humans who Love Them

*heli*ographica

For information:
Heliographica
2261 Market St., #504
San Francisco, CA 94114
www.heliographica.com

ISBN 1-933037-38-5

Printed in the United States of America

CONTENTS

DEDICATION

This book is dedicated to all the animals in the world, whether they are loved as a family member, secure and warm in loving homes; or suffering at the end of a short leash with no comforting words, or no warm bed in which to feel secure day after day.

The authors of this book provide loving homes, and find themselves aghast at the suffering of those they can't personally care for. It is our hope that humans who read these stories can recognize an animal's suffering, whether it is owned by a relative or neighbor, and take steps to rectify the situation. If this book can save one animal's life, or end the suffering and loneliness of one that needs a loving home, we will be happy.

* * * * *

My friend Julie Tangen says, "Cows are supposed to moo all day and sheepdogs are supposed to herd. The rooster sits on the fencepost to greet the day, his job to provide a cock-a-doodle-doo!!!

"Dogs bark, and kitties wag their tails in that way they have as they watch the birds. The birds sing with delight when we provide fresh water. Horses bring in the spring with crazy bucks and gallops over the moist ground, whinnying to one another with delight."

And to our furred and feathered loved ones who've passed over the animals' Rainbow Bridge, she says, "Bless you little guys – run and trot in heaven. We will come. That's one thing we can be pretty sure of."

UNCONDITIONAL LOVE

Pet Tales By The Humans Who Love Them

Compiled by Avie Townsend
with
Contributing Authors:

Beth Blair
Alan Campbell
Tricia Draper
Sandy Williams Driver
Diane Clover Evans
Tova Gabrielle
Deborah Hill
Roberta Beach Jacobson
Amy Jenkins
Barbara Jennison
Heide A.W. Kaminski
Kristen Dreyer-Kramer
Ginny Mastondrea
Nina Osier
Dana Smith-Mansell
Kimberly Stauder
Marilyn Ure
Barbara Williamson-Wood

DRAWINGS BY:

Diane Clover Evans
Heidi Kaminski
Dana Smith-Mansell

INTRODUCTION

By Avis Townsend

Working at a veterinary office for the past two years, I've seen it all—the good, the bad and the ugly. I thought people who took their dogs to the vet were kind, caring, loving pet owners. Little did I know that many only go because they are forced to, because the dog is half dead or the cat is exploding with pain from a urinary blockage, or that the rabies shot is overdue and the cops are beating down their door.

I was appalled at the things I saw. I wanted to write a book, hoping to educate the idiots, but soon I realized the idiots would not be the ones to read a how-to book on pet care. Idiots don't care.

However, I also saw caring folks—people who cried when they found their pets were dying of cancer, people who said they'd spend anything if we could keep their animal alive. I also saw heartbroken folks whose animals were dying because of their owners' faultless ignorance. Dogs falling out of the backs of pickup trucks were one of the most common causes of death or injury. It's a macho thing for a guy to have his big dog riding in the back of his truck, scarf on its neck, enjoying the breeze. But it only takes one bump, one quick hit of the brakes, for the dog to fly out of the box and into the path of another car, or under the wheels of his owner's truck. And those tied in the back can hang themselves.

I helped unwanted animals go to rescue agencies. I found homes for abandoned kittens. While at the vet office, I discovered ailments I had no idea existed, and how they could have been prevented with a little common knowledge.

I knew I had to educate people. But how? I decided to do this anthology, hoping people would pick it up and read a story here and there, and maybe a light bulb would go off in their own heads, and they'd realize there is something they can do to help their furry, fuzzy or feathered friends.

A passage from the Bible, which was eventually turned into a movie, has stuck with me for decades…"Bless the beasts and the children." We have to protect them both. Fortunately, more and more agencies are being developed to help children, but how many communities can afford to help pets as they should? And how can someone realize that animals are living creatures offering us unconditional love, at the mercy of our care giving? How can we teach them that animals aren't "a dime a dozen" and should be cherished, adoring fur-people seeking comfort from their humans? Is responsibility learned, or must it be taught? Is there something inside of us that knows right from wrong, or are we taught by the school of hard knocks?

Growing up in the 1950's and 1960's, I witnessed many things I couldn't understand, and I remember all of them as if they happened last week.

For instance, when I was three I was standing in the yard with my parents when my uncle pulled up to the curb in his old jalopy. I noticed the shotgun on the front seat as he opened the door. He got out, all six-feet, seven inches of him, dressed in overalls, a faded flannel shirt, and topped with a tattered straw hat. He grinned broadly, his smile showing the many spaces where there were no teeth, and he walked to the trunk in about three strides. When it opened, he pulled out six brown rabbits, their back legs tied together with twine, and I remember them being stretched out long, not curled and puffy like the bunnies on display in the local department stores at Easter time. Also, their stomachs were hallowed out— wide open—showing nothing but bloody emptiness.

"Mom." I tugged on the hem of my mother's housedress, frowning and staring at the strange-looking animals. Their eyes were open but they didn't communicate. I was confused. Finally, she looked at me and I motioned for her to lean down, like I had a secret. Instead, I asked her, "What's wrong with the bunnies' tummies?"

She laughed. "They don't have any tummies, silly, they're dead."

No one paid attention when I quietly asked, "But why?" They were too busy praising his expert shooting and talking about rabbit stew. I was still confused. Why were they dead? Why did he take out their stomachs? Why did they stare into space from empty eyes? Did they hurt from having no stomachs? Did he kill them with his gun? But why? And why didn't anyone think this scene was bizarre?

I never forgot that pile of dead rabbits. Even now, every time I see a tattered straw hat, I remember the lifeless bodies lying inside my uncle's trunk. And I still don't understand why they had to die. For food? Isn't that what supermarkets are for?

Shortly after the bunny incident, my parents and I moved to the country, and they bought me a beagle puppy named Jeffrey. At the time, I didn't associate the paradox of beagles and rabbits. I just knew I had a cute puppy. He wasn't allowed in the house, so I could only see him on good days when the weather was nice, when I could go out to the yard and pet him as he sat tied to his house by a short chain.

We only had him a few days when his chain broke and he ran into the road, killed instantly by a passing car. The lady who hit him offered to throw his body over the bank into a nearby creek, but my mother said no thanks, she'd bury him herself. I silently witnessed the whole thing–Jeffrey running in the road, the screeching of brakes, the woman offering to throw him in the water. I was numb, not understanding the meaning of death, not even after seeing the dead bunnies. Fortunately, I didn't see Jeffrey's body. My mother somehow sheltered me from that image. But she didn't shelter me from a conversation she had with my grandmother after Jeffrey was discreetly disposed of.

"I thought she'd be crying hysterically and all upset over it, but it doesn't seem to phase her at all. I guess she's hard-hearted."

I knew she was talking about me, and I knew the puppy had died, but I didn't know him well enough to grieve. I was barely five, and I'd had no time to form an attachment, not to mention comprehend that dead meant gone away forever. As far as I knew he'd be back someday. Maybe he was with the people we got him from. Maybe he'd return.

But my mother's words bothered me. Why wasn't I "fazed"? Was I supposed to be? And what exactly was "fazed?" Or "hard-hearted" for that matter. Both terms seemed insulting. No, I never cried, but I thought about Jeffrey for years, still picturing his floppy ears, the white blaze on his face, the soft jowls that surrounded his mouth. I cried later, when I was much older, when the realization of what happened finally hit home.

When I was six, I watched my friend Donna cry pitifully after her dog was killed in the road. Her brother came and picked him up by his legs and carried him away. A spaniel, his head dangled and curly ears flopped as Donna's brother carried his lifeless body upside-down to their house. Watching her, I remembered Jeffrey and how I didn't cry, and here she was crying hysterically. I wondered if there was something wrong with me.

My mother had taken a picture of Jeffrey when he first arrived. Years later, after she died and I was going through her things, I found the photo. When I looked into those eyes in the photograph, I sobbed for hours, apologizing to him for not grieving when I was a child, for not being phased, and for being so hard-hearted.

But back to my childhood, there were so many unanswered questions. Why did the lady want to throw Jeffrey in the creek? Why did Uncle Albert like to shoot the bunnies? Nothing made any sense.

We got Skippy when I was seven. He was a wonderful cat—orange tabby with a white chest and feet. He let me dress him up in baby clothes and push him around in my doll buggy. I loved him dearly. A few months after we had him, he disappeared. I went outside and called him and called some more, but he never came.

I cried, I fretted, I stewed. I couldn't eat. I was devastated. I was finally "fazed." And my hard heart was broken.

Finally my father could take it no more. "The cat is gone. We took it to a farm. It was pregnant and we don't need a bunch of kittens around here."

"What farm? Where?" I was flabbergasted. Apparently Skippy was a girl and about to have babies. What was wrong with having kittens?

My mother was furious with him. "Why did you tell her? She didn't need to know."

He shook his head. "I disagree. She has to learn what real life is. The cat will be happy at a farm, eating mice, having lots of room to run."

"Go get him… her! Go bring her back. Take me with you." I hung on his arm, but no amount of crying or pleading would get him to change his mind. It was then I decided: When I grew up, I would have all the animals I wanted. They would live in the house, and I'd never let them go. I would never own a gun, and I'd never make an animal live in a dog house. And I'd make sure they'd never get hit by a car.

I'm grown up now—with kids that are also grown up, and four grandchildren to enjoy. The kids all have their own pets, but they can't hold a candle to the number I have. At this writing, I own six dogs, eleven cats, and six equine creatures, including a donkey, a miniature horse, a Shetland pony and a miniature draft horse, plus two regular horses in a barn my husband and I built when we were in our fifties. Most of my creatures are rescues, because I can't bear to see an animal suffer, either from abuse or loneliness.

I took the part time job at my local vet clinic, partly to help animals, partly to help pay my vet bills, but always with the thoughts that all pet owners were as conscientious as I was—that they'd love their animals no matter what.

Wow! I was hit in the head with the hammer of life. There are people who'd rather shoot a kitten than have it put to sleep humanely—or slam it in the head with a shovel. There are people who just plain shouldn't own animals.

I'm hoping to make this anthology a learning experience for everyone who reads it. Perhaps it will help one person see the error of his ways. Perhaps it will help one person to have the courage to report a neighbor to the authorities for abusing or neglecting pets. Perhaps it will bring a tear to the eye or a smile on someone's face, and make them want to go out and find a pet to care for and nurture, whether it be for the few years it has left, or a lifetime.

I am an animal lover, as are the people who contributed to this book. We feel pets have as much right as people to be treated fairly. They have feelings, they love us unconditionally, even when we leave them out in the cold, ignore them or snarl at them because we've had a bad day.

It is my wish that this book, and the many heartwarming stories in it, helps save the lives of many animals, both large and small, which need a helping hand by someone who cares.

The following stories are true and written by me and a group of writers from across the world. I've told you my history. The other writers' biographies will be listed at the end of their tales. And the photos of most of their pets will be included with their stories.

A DOG NAMED FEEN

By Avis Townsend

We connected the first time I saw her. She came trotting down the road like a blonde goddess, fluffy tail flowing in the light breeze. She was very thin, ribs sticking out like a xylophone, but she had an air of confidence about her. As she trotted by, I stepped out to the front porch and called to her. She stopped, inquisitive, and turned to look at me.

"How are you, pretty girl?" I cooed to her.

She thrust her nose in the air with the stance of a howling wolf and gave me three trilling *a-rooo's*. Then she turned and continued her trot down the road.

"She's going to be dead soon, just like the rest of them," my husband said.

"Why? Who owns her?" I asked him.

"She belongs to those horrible people down the street."

"Not the Blacks?" I shouted. *The horrible Blacks.* In trouble with the police all the time, their children had been taken away by child protection more than once. They had all sorts of dogs in and around their house, and I'd been told they shot off guns inside the home.

I became sad, watching her trot away, wondering how long she'd live. She was doomed to be hit by a car, or killed by her owners. Such an elegant dog should never have to live with such people, I thought.

It wasn't long before my prediction was realized. One sunny day when I was taking an afternoon walk, the blonde dog was lying in the vacant field next to the Black's house. There were fat, fuzzy puppies drinking from her. As she lay on her side, she tried to get up to tend to them, but all she could do was lift her head. She was injured.

I rushed home and called the town hall. They said they'd received several calls and the dog catcher would be by soon to take her and the puppies. I felt for her, knowing she would probably be put to sleep, but at least she'd be out of pain and away from the Blacks.

The next day, I walked by and she was still lying there. It had rained all night and she was soaked. Furious, I rushed back home and called the dog catcher. He said someone would be coming by the next day.

"That makes three days in a field with injuries. Can't you come now?"

"Too busy," he said. "Maybe she'll die and the owners can take care of the body."

I was mortified. Didn't people care? Just like when I was growing up, animals were treated like disposables. Well, not *this* animal, not if I had anything to say about it. Grabbing the telephone book in one hand and the phone in the other, I called our local dog rescue lady, Emmy Altbach. She would know what to do. Emmy was our town's patron saint of animals.

When I told her the story, Emmy was livid. "I called the town hall days ago. How can they let her lie there like that?"

Then she asked me if I would meet her at the Black's house. We would get the dog and take it to a veterinarian to be euthanized. She would find homes for the puppies. I agreed to help, and within minutes I was by the dog's side and she pulled up in her car, sputtering and muttering at the inhumanity of man.

"Look at these sweet puppies. Why, this dog is only a puppy herself, and the owners let her get pregnant." Still sputtering, Emmy pulled a large plaid blanket from the back seat and carried it to the Black's door. She stood there, pounding the door with her first, a look of determination on her face, her jaw set from anger.

Finally, Mr. Black, eyes filled with sleep, opened the door.

Emmy shook her finger at him. "Shame on you, letting your dog suffer like that. And shame on you for letting her have these puppies. We're taking her away, and you're going to help us."

"What do you want me to do?" he asked, looking at her like she was an annoying bug that needed to be flicked from his space.

"You'll pick her up and put her in the car."

Black scowled. "I ain't picking her up—she might try to bite me."

"She *should* bite you for how you've treated her. She's your dog, if you don't want me to call the police on you for animal abuse, you'll pick her up and put her in the car."

Black begrudgingly walked over and picked up the dog. Emmy told me to sit in the back seat, and she put the blanket across my lap. Then she instructed Black to put the dog on the blanket. As he did, Emmy picked up the four puppies gathered around her ankles and loaded them into the back seat with us.

As we drove to the veterinarian, Emmy explained that the Blacks had recently raised beagles, and every one of them had been killed in the past two weeks, including both parents and five puppies, because the Blacks allowed them to run wild.

"Some people should not be allowed to have dogs," she said.

As we drove along, the dog looked up at me with huge brown eyes. She had a large cut on her left leg, but other than that, I could see no injuries. Yet she seemed paralyzed. She whimpered to her puppies now and then, but she seemed quite calm.

"This dog is really too nice to be put to sleep," I said. "For someone to lie there for days, no food or water except for the rain, she has a great temperament."

"Yes, it's a shame," Emmy said, "but we have so many dogs looking for homes. However, if you said *you'd* take her, we could see how badly she's injured, and if it's not life threatening, you could have her."

Oh, dear, I could see my husband if I came home with another dog. We already had three. Yet, as I looked into those big doe eyes, I knew I couldn't just let her die.

"Okay, I'll pay for any surgery she might need. If the vet says she'll recover, I'll take her."

As it was, the injuries weren't that bad. She had a dislocated hip and a few bumps and bruises. The doctor operated, spaying her at the same time he repaired her hip. The puppies were partially weaned and were only drinking from her for the extra nourishment not given them by the Blacks. Emmy found homes for them immediately.

After a few days, I was allowed to take the dog home. I re-named her Fawn, because she looked like a deer, and my husband didn't object to the adoption, much to my surprise. The doctor said she'd probably live well for seven years, then arthritis would settle into her scarred joints and she'd have no quality of life. I figured seven years were better than no years, so I took her home with that in mind.

It was difficult at first, with Fawn trying to go back to her old home to find her babies, and the Black children stopping by all the time, wondering when they could take "Honey" home. That's the name they had given her.

Fortunately, it was only a few weeks before the Blacks were evicted and forced to move, so I didn't have to see them again. They had caused so much damage inside their rental home, the owners bulldozed it down when they moved out.

Eventually, Fawn settled in well, and I began taking her and the other dogs for long walks in the county park, which was a short distance away.

After a few years, we moved to another town, and we acquired a family of cats to go with our family of dogs. Fawn, we found out, was somewhat of a nurse. Whenever one of the animals had a hurt, whether it be an abscess, a torn toenail, or any form of cut, Fawn would whine and cry and push them all over with her nose, making me go over and check things out.

She was incredible at finding little injuries. Fortunately, I was able to take the pets to the doctors before things got too bad, or too expensive. On several occasions, she'd found sores on the cats that could have turned into abscesses. We caught them in time, treating them before things got out of hand.

One day she carried home a baby rabbit in her mouth. She didn't hurt it, but she had found it somewhere and brought it to me. I called a rehabilitator and took the bunny there. While waiting to find someone to take it to, Fawn danced and pranced around the carrier I'd placed it in, worried about the little charge she brought home to care for.

We began calling her Nurse Fawn Black, or Nurse Black. She had long ago become a beloved member of the family, and as her seventh year rolled around, I began to fret, watching for signs of arthritis the vet had warned us about, but there were none. She was silly, and pranced and danced happily. Eventually Nurse Black got shortened to Feen, or Feenie. Most of our dogs started out with one name, and ended up with several nicknames by the time they left this earth. Once Fawn became Feen, however, she kept the name for the rest of her life.

New visitors to the house would ask us where we got the puppy. At first it surprised us, but then we got used to the question. She never seemed to age. She was always full of energy and could run at top speed with no signs of pain.

Her happiest time was when we moved into our last home, a fifty-acre farm with hills and trails for her to explore. She loved following me to the horse barn and watching me while I did my chores. As she got older it was our ritual, morning and night, to go to the barn together, Feen's nose always close to my leg. When I put the horses in, Feen stood by the gate. Once the last one was put away, she'd open the gate with her paw and come down the aisle, knowing she was safe from being stepped on.

Unfortunately, as the saying goes "All good things must come to an end." As she entered her sixteenth year, she began slowing down. Her eyes had become clouded with cataracts, and her hearing was all but gone. I knew she didn't have much time left, and I hoped she would die in her sleep so I wouldn't have to take her to the vet's office for euthanasia. One morning I woke up and she was curled up on the bed, quite cold, and I thought she had died. But when I reached out to pet her lifeless body, she woke up and looked at me through cloudy eyes. She wasn't ready to go just yet.

She still went out to the barn with me, but occasionally she'd become disoriented and walk in a different direction, and I'd have to wave my arms so she could see where I was. I had to begin tying her outside, because she couldn't see or hear cars coming down the road anymore. Although she never went in the road when she could see, I'd find her standing in the center many times after she lost her vision. She didn't seem to mind being tied out off and on during the day, as long as she could still follow me to do errands morning and night.

I took her to the veterinarian for a geriatric checkup, and one of the tests showed she was in the early stages of kidney failure. I put her on special food, and the doctor told me to watch for danger signs. She would begin urinating many times a day, they said, and she'd get dehydrated. Her fur would become ratty looking, and she'd lose her enthusiasm for life.

As more time went by, she slept almost continually and was going to the bathroom most of her waking moments. Her back legs would give out sometimes when she stood up, and she seemed to be confused, always looking for me when I was out of sight. I'd have to make myself known to her when I came in the room. The time was drawing near to let her go.

I made my husband take her. I couldn't do it myself. I didn't want to remember my dear friend lying on a table with a needle in her vein, life ebbing away. I didn't want to be the traitor—the killer—the murderer. She would feel my heartache, I reasoned, and I didn't want her more upset than she'd be already.

I scheduled three separate appointments and cancelled them all before the final one was kept. Each time I'd think her quality of life was slipping away, but then she'd bounce back and run around like a puppy again. But on her last day, she gave me the message—it was time. I called and made the appointment, and told hubby it was time to take her for her final ride.

I got up and did my morning chores, and Feen came along as usual, but her heart wasn't in it. When she stood up to go out, she fell, and when I put out the horses she didn't try to come through the gate.

I walked her down the lane to the glade she loved to run in, but she just stood there by my leg, not interested in anything. I bent down and gave her a hug, and then I began to cry. When we walked back toward the house, my husband was there waiting, Feen's leash in his hand.

He loaded her into the car and they drove away. I sobbed, knowing I'd never see my wonderful friend again.

It was over. Sixteen years with a faithful friend. Sixteen years of fabulous memories, photos in the album, her leash hanging in its spot by the back door.

When he got home, my husband said it went well. She didn't cry, he said, she just went to sleep. I cried again, and I'm crying now. I know I'll never get over losing Feen. She was my best friend. Now and then I'll look for a dog that resembles her but no one has ever come close. When God made her, he broke the mold.

I still think of the first time I saw her, trotting down the road, seeming so happy to be alive. She brought a great deal of joy to our lives, and I doubt I'll ever find another dog like her.

A GIRL THING

By Beth Blair

Our second Chesapeake Bay Retriever Mako is a beautiful dog with dark brown coloring, a broad chest, and huge paws. The epitome of a Chessie, she is a working dog that doesn't stop "working" until the sun sets. She dives in the pool and moves huge rocks all over the yard—rocks that I have to use two hands to pick up—while our other Chessie lounges around watching her.

When Mako came to live with us, she was still working toward her show championship. Already the mother of one litter, we decided that as soon as she received all of her points we would be making a trip to the veterinarian's office to ensure no more litters would be coming from her. Until then, we would have to just deal with what comes along with having a fertile dog. We prepared and bought the proper diapers, pads, and baby gate so she would stay in the tiled kitchen.

A few months after joining our family, and right on time, Mako went into heat. I, being on the road for work, was called by my husband and told "it" had started. "It" wouldn't have been a big deal except the diaper part wasn't going so well.

"She won't let me put the diaper on her," my husband said over the phone. "Please, hurry home."

When I arrived home the next day my six-year-old, ninety-pound Chessie was sad and despondent. Her ears were drooping and her tail was still. A diaper was hanging low and barely fastened on.

When my husband saw the look on my face he said, "I tried. She won't stand still for me. Will you try?"

I removed Mako's sagging diaper and let her go outside to take care of business. A little while later she was at the door, ready to return inside. When I let her in she saw the diaper and took her place in front of me. I placed a new pad in the cloth dog-diaper and attempted to put her tail through the hole. Instead, her tail remained tucked. She stood glaring at Bear, our male Chessie, and my husband. When she glanced back at me with her hopeless eyes I knew.

"I think you better leave the room," I told my husband, "and take Bear with you."

As the two trudged upstairs Mako's ears returned to their normal position and her tense body relaxed. Her tail returned to its normal position and when I put her tail through the hole it started to wag. Next, I fastened the Velcro securely on each side. Within seconds the mission was complete. I called the boys down.

My husband walked down the stairs with a look of shock on his face. "How did you do it so fast?" He asked. "It took me an hour to even get her tail through the hole and she kept running in circles."

I patted Mako's head as she looked up at me. "It's girl thing."

Author's Bio: Elizabeth L. Blair is a freelance writer based in Tucson, AZ where she happily lives with her husband, two stepson, and two Chesapeake Bay Retrievers, Mako and Bear. Her work has appeared in publications such as the *Christian Science Monitor*, *Chicken Soup for the Bride's Soul*, *The Dollar Stretcher*, and many more. You can contact her through email at elblair99@yahoo.com

A LITTLE COMMON SENSE FOR PET OWNERS

By an anonymous rescuer and breeder

So you want a new pet? Where should you get it? You've heard about the horrors of puppy and kitten mills. Pet shops buy from millers. If you get a purebred, will it be inbred too much, and be so high strung you can't deal with it?

Puppy mill rescues, purebred dogs and cats from an *ethical* breeder—they could all have faults and defects of some kind, or breed characteristics and traits. There is no guarantee. Too many people look for perfection.

It is true, breeders should strive to breed healthy animals, but pet owners also have a responsibility to provide optimum care for their pet. There will always be people who will not neuter or spay mix breeds or the purebreds that should not be bred, resulting in thousands of puppies and kittens euthanized each day. Also, sneaky and unethical pet owners are out there lying to breeders.

Many breeders have the buyers sign a form, stating they will have the baby neutered when it's age-appropriate. But, unless they follow up on a weekly basis, the breeders have no assurance that the pet-quality animal they just sold are not being bred by the new owner to make money. The only answer is to keep the pet until it's older, and get it neutered yourself, but then people will say they don't want an animal that old.

The breeders have a reputation to maintain, and irresponsible pet owners exist just as irresponsible breeders exist. True, no cat or dog is perfect, but ethical breeders strive to breed healthy pets and have their studs, bitches and queens (female cats) genetically tested. In dogs it's for hip dysplasia and other ailments. In Zots and Persian cats it is for kidney ailment, or PDK. A lot of controversy exists in the cat world on who is to "blame" for the extreme faced Persians and Zots and problems that come with it, and Siamese cats, also. I personally prefer the "open" face because the health problems were minimal to non existent. Bull Dogs, Pekingese, and Pugs I'm sure have the same problems or similar. The solution is equally ethical, responsible breeding and equally ethical responsible pet ownership.

I'm guilty of adopting shelter dogs and cats and would probably adopt a mill dog rescue if I felt I could save the animal. I know my cats are well bred and healthy, pet quality because in me the breeder found a good home for a cat that didn't meet the breeding program, so everyone wins. If your desire is to have a purebred pet, and you believe health, temperament and confirmation are important, support the *good* breeders that strive to produce quality puppies and kittens!

Not every purebred dog or cat will be show quality, and for some minor fault they may need to be placed as a pet. Be willing to pay the breeders for their time, line and efforts. That is how you establish a good rapport and working relationship. Are there breeders that lie, and misrepresent and produce poor quality? You bet, and I have been a victim even though I did my homework. Do some breeders falsify papers, and cheat people? You bet.

Do some pet owners lie and breed their dog with or without papers after promising to spay/neuter? You bet. Do some go through pets like used tissue and discard them, abuse them, neglect them, not feed them? You Bet. Sadly for the animals and God's creatures, innocent trusting life put into man's care, they suffer because of man's cruelty and inhumanity. I have rescued, but I know ahead of time my chances are I will be caring for a sickly or unhealthy animal. I'm willing to take the challenge and put the effort in it and my expectations are not high. It is probably wiser to get a healthy pet from a reputable breeder, and cheaper in the long run

I rescue because I'm a sucker and arguably stupid, to some degree, and soft headed and an easy touch, but I know pretty well what to expect. My advice is to buy a healthy puppy from a good breeder and support them and their efforts. Where else do purebreds that are healthy and quality come from?

I don't begrudge the rescues, they also do a good service for these poor dogs that need and deserve a good home and there is plenty of room for both. My dog gets along with the indoor cats. He would probably kill an outside cat that came in the yard. He would probably kill one of my inside cats if they ventured outside. As good as he is, he has a prey drive. I see it and I recognize it.

I have heard of people who have a large dog and want to get a kitten, but they know their dog would kill it. They want to break the dog of that habit, so they bring kitten after kitten into the house, testing the dog to see if it will adapt, and over and over the dog kills the kitten. This is cruelty. It is also teaching the dog to kill, rather than getting the dog to become used to cats. These people need to realize that they will never have a cat as long as the large dog is alive.

Strive to be the best you can be as a pet owner or breeder. Honor your word. In some cases, a pet has to be euthanized. I have been there. I have even had rescues that didn't make it. In some situations that are terminal and your pet is in pain, please don't be selfish and think of yourself without your pet. Think of the good years, the love, the good times and how your pet still depends on you to make the right choices and decisions, and don't let your pet suffer and languish in pain.

"Taking him home to die" is not an end to suffering — it only prolongs it. Let your pet leave this earth with dignity, and don't prolong his suffering to ease your grief at losing him.

ABOUT STARTING OVER   MR. B AND ME

By Barbara Jennison

We began by putting one foot in front of the other. Mr. B. actually put one paw in front of the other. I couldn't explain to him why our lives had changed but I think he knew. One day Pop was there and the next he wasn't. To add to his confusion, his canine mother, Millie, whom we had tended to the end of her life, left us later. Our whole world had turned upside down.

For weeks, he sat at the door and waited for Pop to return from work. For days, he went to Millie's pillow and sniffed around and turned questioning eyes to me.

I felt as though he wanted to know, "What have you done with them? They're the most important parts of our lives!"

I struggled with my decisions about my Mr. B. and my own lives. How could we live here where we'd spent so many years with our significant others and now they were gone? Was it even fair to try? For myself, I knew I couldn't stay where my husband had spent so many hours in pain and retain my sanity. Mr. B, actually Jerry's Barachou Man, didn't understand why we were there and they were not. Time couldn't possibly take care of our pain.

I knew it didn't matter to our daughters. They hadn't grown up in the house. The only thing the house did for we humans was bring pain and an aching loneliness. Somehow, I thought it might be the same for Mr. B, my little Shih Tzu. After we had rattled around wallowing in our misery for a couple of months, I made my decision public. My four girls agreed with me. I should change my surroundings.

We all wondered if Mr. B. would adjust. As I packed things away and drove across town, I know he was confused as to why we were putting things we used in storage. But like a dutiful child, which he'd become to me, he went along with my actions. When the final items were moved, I'm not sure he understood that we would not be returning. This was our own home, just his and mine. New surroundings hopefully would bring new peace.

If I'd had any doubts, his reaction to the area erased them from my mind. He loved it and seems to love it more each day, especially going outside and romping in our yard. When I get out his leash and my mailbox keys, he does his happy little dance as I try to secure the connector to his collar. Then we trot to the mailbox while he happily sniffs to see if his boundary marks are still there. If they aren't, he re-marks them all the way around our lot.

Lately, he's discovered a patch of edible plants. He looks back at me and we go where he leads me. I don't know if it's a treat or a natural remedy for him but if it makes him happy, I don't mind. The area just happens to be where I had my glider placed. I can sit there with a book. He's not upset at being tethered if I'm close by.

We're learning to adjust to being alone, the two of us. He, who I had worried would have a hard time adjusting, is enjoying being an "only child." He also doesn't mind not having to help with Millie. She was blind, going deaf and a little senile. Mr. B would take her by the scuff if she was headed into trouble. He would come get me if there was something she needed me to do.

He is smart but he doesn't open doors. Not that he couldn't, but I don't feel it would be a good idea. Who knows what new mischief he could get into!

He sets our rising and going to bed time. He reminds me when it's time to eat. He even thinks he knows when I've been at the keyboard too long.

I can ask him what he wants and through his own language, he tells me. My oldest daughter is amused at his little potty-dance.

Yes, my life has changed drastically. My husband and I had been together for more than 45 years. We had been married nearly all that time.

Mr. B. and I have been together all his life. I helped Millie deliver the litter he was part of.

I know that down the road, one of us will have to adjust to another change, but right now, we're just putting one foot and one paw in front of the other on our new journey through life. We're trying to make the most of what time we have.

Author's Bio: Barbara Jennison has been writing most of her life. At present, she is concentrating on articles and short stories, although she has finished novels and is looking to be published. She is a member of Romance Writers of America and a local writers group in San Angelo, Texas.

A PLACE FOR KITTY

By Tricia Draper

"Grandma, can we go see Kitty?" I asked, a hopeful expression on my face.

"Sure, Tricia," Grandma said, as she tucked my small hand in hers. The front door creaked as it opened. It always made the same noise. I ruffled the little yellow balls on the door curtains, as I had done thousands of times before. I held the heavy white metal screen door for her. We somberly walked down the two porch steps and turned towards the back yard.

We were quiet on our trip to visit Kitty. It had only been two days since we had last taken this trip, but it seemed longer to me. I could feel the hot Iowa summer sun beating down on my freckled seven-year-old face. My straight long brown hair was hanging loosely around my shoulders.

The air smelled sweet from Grandma's garden growing a few yards away. I loved the beautiful flowers and how pretty they always looked. It was so amazing to me that she could plant seeds in the ground, and have them grow to be flowers and food. There were neat little rows in back of the flowers containing different types of fruits and vegetables. My grandma could do anything in the whole world.

We walked around the corner of the house, and there stood the little forest. I knew Kitty was in there. As we neared the forest, I saw a little squirrel dropped his nut and scurry up a nearby tree. He had a scared but frustrated look in his eyes. Cardinals and blue jays squawked at us, letting us know their disapproval of having to fly away.

"Are you all right?" Grandma asked, as she squeezed my hand. "We can come back later if you want to."

"I'm okay. I have to do this for Kitty. I promised her I would," I replied. I was trying my best to be brave. The forest was really just a small cluster of trees, but every time I looked at it, I was a little scared. From the outside it looked dark, damp, and gloomy. But, something changed as soon as you stepped inside.

I stepped into the interior, and a rush of cool, clean air washed over my body. It felt good to be out of the blazing heat. I stepped on a twig and jumped, as the snapping sound echoed through the trees. Grandma knocked down a spider's web that was in her way. I thought about the Charlotte's Web movie I had seen at school. I wondered if that spider was upset about loosing her home. A few more timid steps, and we were there.

In the middle of the little forest was a clearing. Here was the final resting place of my beloved kitten, Kitty. One of Grandma's cats had a litter of kittens, and she'd been the smallest one born. No one expected her to live. No one, that is, except me. I fed her with a baby bottle, kept her warm, and took her everywhere with me. We were best friends.

Suddenly, after two weeks of tender loving care she stopped eating, and became weaker and weaker. Grandma said there was nothing we could do for her, but that didn't ease my pain. I awoke one rainy morning, but Kitty did not. The weather matched my mood: gloomy and sad.

Standing in front of the little wooden cross we had made for her grave, I felt a tear trickle down my cheek. At least I could still come visit her. I knelt down and lay a tiny cluster of blue flowers at the foot of the cross. Surrounded by lovely trees and singing birds, I knew I had picked the perfect place to bury my precious Kitty.

I could taste the salty tears in my mouth as I turned and asked, "Grandma, do you think God is watching over Kitty right now?"

"Yes, honey, I think He is," she said, wiping the tears from her face.

As we walked back to the house, I felt a gentle peace knowing Kitty was in heaven with God. I looked up at the clear blue sky and said a little prayer, thanking God for taking care of Kitty, and for such a wonderful grandma.

Author's Bio: Tricia Draper, author, editor, and freelance journalist, lives in Decatur, TX with her husband and young son. *Angels Among Us*, her first novel, is currently available. Her first book in a children's series, *Bobby Bear Learns to be a Cowboy*, is coming soon. When she's not writing, she loves spending time with her family and her beloved horse. To find out more about her or her work, please visit her site at www.triciadraper.com.

ALWAYS A KITTY, NEVER A CAT

By Kristin Dreyer Kramer

"I hate cats," Dad always grumbled whenever I begged him for a pet. All I wanted was a friend. Both of my brothers had moved out of the house, and there weren't many kids my age in the neighborhood. I just wanted someone to play with. But Dad made it very clear that he didn't want a cat. They shed. They jump on things. And they use the good living room furniture as scratching posts.

But one weekend when I was thirteen—and Dad was out of town—Mom told me about an ad she'd seen in the paper. Someone was giving away free kittens. "Let's get one," she said with a smile.

I had no idea how Dad would react when he came home to find a kitten in the house—but I wasn't about to question Mom's idea, either. So Mom and I drove out to a little house in the country to find our kitten. By the time we got there, there was just one left. She was a beautiful, tiny runt—a gray tabby with orange calico patches and spotless white paws and bright green eyes. Mom and I both fell in love with the tiny bundle of fur, so we picked her up and took her home.

Cats, I've found, know exactly which people in the room are cat-lovers and which aren't. They single out the doubters—and then they proceed to follow them around, flaunting all of their charm and adorable-ness. So as soon as Dad came home, our new kitten attached herself to him—in more ways than one. While he was standing in the kitchen, telling us about his weekend, she scampered up to him and clawed her way up his jeans to get a closer look. Dad looked down to see the kitten hanging from the waist of his jeans, looking up at him, and he just muttered, "It's gonna have to be declawed."

From the very beginning, Mischief (Misti for short—but we always just called her Kitty) followed Dad wherever he went. She trotted behind him as he went from room to room. She jumped onto his lap whenever he sat in his favorite chair.

"Still hate cats, Dad?" we'd ask him as he played with his new friend.

"She's just a kitten," he'd say. "Kittens are okay. It's *cats* I hate."

But as Kitty grew older, Dad only loved her more. She may have been my best friend—my real, live teddy bear, as I often called her—but she was Dad's *baby*. He played with her. He watched TV with her. He talked to her—always in baby talk. Each morning when he got up, the first thing he'd do was find Kitty. "Good morning, Kitty," he'd say as he lifted the barely-awake but already purring bundle that had come to greet him. And together they'd walk through the house, look out the window, and have their morning chat before Dad had to get ready for work.

Sometimes, when Dad was walking through the house with Kitty in his arms, Mom and I would smile and say, "I hate cats," mimicking Dad's old gruff statement. He'd just grin and laugh a little and walk away, still cuddling the creature that would always just be "Kitty"—who never, apparently, grew to be a cat.

Author's Bio: Kristin Dreyer Kramer is proud to be a Cat Person. She's also a freelance writer, columnist, and the editor-in-chief of *NightsAndWeekends.com* Kristin lives in Massachusetts with her husband, Paul—who *isn't* a Cat Person. For more about Kristin, visit her web site at nightsandweekends.com/kdk or contact her at kdk@nightsandweekends.com.

BUFFY – DIARY OF A LOVING RESCUE

By Ginny Mastondrea

[Editor's note: *Wire-haired fox terriers are a perky little breed, and not everyone should own one. They are feisty, bouncy, find ways to get into lots of trouble, and are sometimes more intelligent than their owners. But they have a worldwide network of owners, giving advice to other owners, comparing notes on their pets, and it's a great support system.*

There is a Wirehair Fox Terrier Rescue organization, which offers abused or abandoned pets to new owners, and applicants must meet various criteria, almost as if they were adopting a child, to get one.

Ginny Mastondrea of Hackettstown, New Jersey, passed the requirements for adoption and picked up Buffy in the winter of 2003.

The following is her story:]

It is another snowy day here in northwest New Jersey. It's a small storm, we are expected to get about five inches. This is on top of the six inches that is left from the blizzard a while ago. My entire yard is ice so there is nothing better than taking some time to recount my original almost fifty-year-old Heart-in-the-Mouth story.

I grew up in Jersey City in the fifties. We lived in a six-room apartment and did not have a yard. I was eleven years old and we had never had a dog. My mother had dogs as a child, one a toy fox terrier. We probably would never have received a dog from a rescue group. As it was, my father bought me a wire-haired fox terrier puppy for my eleventh birthday with the understanding that it was my responsibility to feed, walk, bathe, brush, and train the dog. I would receive some help with the walking at night but otherwise she was mine to care for. I had no

43

doubt that my father was a man of his word and so I learned responsibility. It was wonderful!

One weekend my aunt came to visit, so I was dispossessed from my room and sent to sleep on the Simmons pull-out couch in the living room. The next morning my father helped me unmake the bed and fold it back into a couch. I had fed my puppy, Sherry, poached egg and dry toast for breakfast, and after making my bed, I went to walk her. My brother and his friends had been in and out of the house all morning. I lived on the second floor and there was the door to our apartment, a flight of stairs and then the outside door. Well, I looked all around the house but we could not find Sherry anywhere. Finally, we went outside and searched the neighborhood for hours. to no avail.

Dejected, in tears, my eleven-year-old world in ruins, I sat down on the couch to have a good cry. In the silence, tears streamed down my face, and then I heard her! She was softly scratching inside the couch. Apparently, she had wandered under the sofa bed and my father had closed her in it.

We quickly pulled out the bed, and there she was, no worse for the wear. Fortunately, she was fine. After that, any time we closed the bed up, she ran through the rooms barking. Can't say as I blame her.

And that is how I became a charter member of the Heart in the Mouth Club in 1954. I have periodically renewed my membership throughout the years. Fortunately, each episode always ended happily.

Having entered the world of double dogdom, we are now all four times as crazy. Buffy joined our family on January 24, 2003. My husband Bob and I each wondered how Buffy would interact with Catie, our nine-month-old wire, who had lived with us since she was a baby?

Bob and I drove half way across Pennsylvania to meet Altha, a volunteer rescuer who had driven across the other half. We were delighted to meet her and have lunch with her. She is a marvelous person, dedicated to making every wirehair fox terrier that passes through her capable, loving hands a little more beautiful. (I say more because all wirehair fox terriers, regardless of circumstance, are beautiful to the heart.) Fortunately for Buffy and me, Buffy had spent the night at Altha's home and received a bed bath, pedicure and loving.

Buffy is a puppy mill brood dog who was born on February 28, 1998. She was given away by the miller because he didn't like her anymore. She allegedly came from a better puppy mill that took care of the animals. Well, when Altha received Buffy, she had dreadlocks three inches long. Her pads were caked with old matted hair and dried feces. Her nails were incredibly long and curling under. And, although Altha respected Buffy too much to say, I'm sure that she must have been pretty odiferous.

Altha bathed her, groomed the knots and mats out, Dremeled those poor little nails a bit, scaled Buffy's teeth a little, cleaned her face and stripped it, transforming Buffy into a dog with lovely markings. [Stripping is a form of clipping used on wire-haired dogs. Rather than shaving, stripping the fur keeps the color alive. Supposedly wires in the wild will rub their bodies against the sides of trees to strip the dead hairs off, and a stripping tool is said to be closest to their natural way of doing things.]

After spending the night in this heavenly atmosphere, Altha drove Buffy to us and passed ownership to us. I lovingly refer to Bob as "The Grinch" because he has valiantly fought to maintain our home as a one dog, one cat residence, but he accompanied me on the long ride, not complaining once.

We put Buffy in her new crate and started to proceed east. Before we were out of the parking lot, Buffy whimpered, and I was instructed to stop the car. Bob took her from the crate and held her in his lap. We know that this is not good policy (Caitie has a seat belt), but our hearts went out to this little girl. She lay in Bob's arms for the entire three-hour ride. We stopped several times to walk her, but to no avail. Buffy was just learning to walk on a leash. She was sweet, but timid; you could not make quick movements around her because she frightened easily. Her tail was down the entire ride.

I had arranged for a vet visit with arguably the best vets in the world. When we entered the office and Buffy saw other dogs, her little tail came up and wagged, and she herself became animated.

The vet said it was clear to see that Buffy had been neglected. Her left upper canine tooth was broken off halfway, the enamel on the back of some of her teeth had been worn off, probably from chewing her wire cage, and she had a fatty tumor or very large cyst on her neck, and her feet were in poor condition, Our vet was disturbed by her nails and the color of her pads. Buffy's ears were also irritated.

She was scheduled for spaying February 11 and would have a dental cleaning, the growth removed and her nails clipped and cauterized. It was necessary for her to receive all her inoculations again because there was no written record. She was also given a test for heartworm. Dr. Chris said that despite her condition she appeared to be in relatively good health, steady heartbeat, clear lungs, etc. She was put on a diet, however, because she was rather overweight, weighing in at more than twenty-three pounds, a bit hefty for a wire-hair. She certainly was an armful.

She and Caitie were introduced, and after some licking and sniffing became wary friends. Buffy ate like a trooper. She was not food aggressive, and she allowed me to remove her full bowl. She and Caitie were separated but she went over to see what Caitie was eating, and tried to join her. After dinner and a walk, she went potty in the yard. However, she came back and peed in the kitchen and then on the living room carpet. She drank a lot of water. Caitie tried to entice her to play, but to no avail. Buffy needed to learn what toys and playing are all about. Caitie was determined to teach her.

Eventually it was time for bed. We were all exhausted from our day. Buffy slept well, I think. I didn't hear her. The following morning she had a good appetite, then she buried a marrow bone in her crate. She peed and pooped outside, then peed upon reentry to house. Over marking, I wondered? She and Caitie growled a little bit at each other—Buffy because Caitie was charging around the room and trying to get her to play. Buffy finally began to run with Caitie. Progress was made. Buffy is an old soul. Although she was not yet five, she had lived a long, unloved life. It is a testament to her gentle spirit and wire heart that she trusted us as much as she did. We could lift her and brush her and pet her and put her in her crate for a rest, etc. She was somewhat afraid if Bob made too quick a movement. We suspect that she may have been beaten by a man. Bob planned to spend the evening with Buffy on his lap watching TV.

It was a privilege to have Buffy in our home to help her transition to her forever home. After only one day she taught us that love truly does heal. After two days I was began to worry that I had made a dreadful mistake by taking this poor creature. I had never fostered before and had no idea how to help this pathetic little dog. I was terrified that I was going to damage her even more by doing the wrong thing.

However, after the end of week two I was delirious with joy. One night, at the end of the second week while I was lying on the floor, Buffy kissed me! She had come so far. She had learned to go upstairs, she learned to play and seek out Caitie to play. She was joyful at mealtime, and she no longer drank vast amounts of water and peed every five minutes. She was dry at night and would go outside, but she still had accidents on the rug. We put down papers and she used them more and more. Buffy was still very shy, however, and did not like to have any part of her body touched, except her face. She jumped two feet high if you touched her body.

She shied away from noises. However, she began making eye contact and followed us from room to room, even to the bathroom. If I gated her in the kitchen for even a few minutes she cried piteously.

I owe almost all of Buffy's progress to Caitie. Caitie has taught her to play. Buffy looks to Caitie for safety. She checks to see that Caitie is okay when Bob and I pick her up. Buffy will be anxious and then smell her from stem to stern when we put her down. Buffy and Caitie share everything, even Patch the cat. They both will chew on different rawhides and then switch. I normally don't like rawhide but Buffy has a strong need to chew and loves the stuff, so Caitie gets to chew too. They share everything but Caitie's toy fox. Buffy has adopted it and sleeps with it. She sometimes carries it from room to room. She will allow Caitie to play tug o' war with it for awhile but then takes it away and will not allow Caitie near it. By the end of week two, I was sure that she was going to be okay. She has the heart and spirit of a true terrier. She is plucky and tough yet gentle and loving. When I lay on the floor with her and Caitie, Buffy came over and sniffed and touched me. It was amazing what a little love and affection will do for these valiant little dogs.

After Buffy had been with us a month, she had been spayed and was doing well. We think the miller gave her up because she was not getting pregnant and was therefore worthless to him. It was our good fortune to be fostering her. She is our first foster and a good-natured gentle dog.

We celebrated Buffy's fifth birthday with doggie cupcakes from the Canine Cafe Bakery. Buffy received a stuffed mouse and Caitie a small puppy. They both enjoyed the cupcakes and we sang Happy Birthday. Buffy wanted me to thank everyone [from the Wire-hair Fox terrier website] for their interest, prayers, gifts, donations, and birthday cards. We were overwhelmed with the wonderful warmth, generosity and love that everyone showed to us, complete strangers.

My prayers are with those who had lost a beloved companion now or in the past. I know that we carry these dear ones forever in our hearts. But God is so good that He made our hearts expandable; there is always heart room for one more.

Caitie gets me up at 4:30 occasionally to potty. Patch sometimes starts to try to get me up at 4:00 AM for breakfast. When I resist, he wakes Caitie up because he knows that if she is up then I am up to potty her. They are all smarter than I am!

After seven weeks had passed, Buffy flowered. In the beginning she was extremely fearful, overweight, skittish, and unattached. In less than two months she had gone through major surgery, learned to live with humans, and began to be housebroken. Slowly, she began to trust, to make eye contact, and allowed us to briefly touch her head and face. Little by little she allowed us to touch other parts of her body and she began to follow us around the house at a safe distance. After seven weeks, she walked in front, beside, or behind us, whatever she felt like doing.

She now looks at us and nuzzles and demands to be petted. She occasionally jumps up by the chair in which we are sitting. She growls and prances and dances for her meals. She plays with the cat, and she mothers and grooms and chastises Caitie. She has taken a nibble on a wicker chest and explores every nook and cranny of the house and yard. Recently, she actually stole a sock! She seems to be progressing rapidly though a long delayed puppy hood.

Buffy will now warily approach strangers, looking them in the eye. She delights in each day and basks in the warmth of our home. We have learned that our hearts are expandable and that there is always room for one more small loving creature. We are incredibly proud to announce that Buffy has adopted us as her forever family. We could not stand to look into those gentle, loving, trusting, brown eyes and think that we would soon part with her. She is happy and content and safe in our home and so she shall always be.

When we first took her in, we thought it would be temporary. We were trying out fosterdom. We always intended to only foster Buffy and then to pass her on to a really good home. Our vet and his receptionist told us that the night we first brought Buffy in, they were laughing at us after we left because we had told them that Buffy would not be staying with us. They knew then (we had only had her for three hours) that she wasn't going anywhere and they were betting on how long it would be before we told them she was ours.

So we prepared an announcement: *Robert and Virginia Mastondrea proudly announce the adoption of their new family member: Buffy Marie Mastondrea, sister to Caitie O'Coleman Mastondrea and their cat Patch.*

What a lovely 60th birthday gift she was for me!

After ten weeks, my husband and I can not believe our luck with Buffy. She is a pure delight. She dances and sings for her breakfast and dinner. She chases the cat and licks his ears and neck. She and Caitie play terrier tag. When Buffy sees Bob and I put our coats on, she begins to wag her tail and dance. She tries to coax us into a car ride. She snuggles in Bob's arms and looks out at the world as it goes by.

Buffy sleeps in her bed with the two stuffed foxes and the fox bits that are left, a canvas snoopy, a pink and white rhino and a little gray mouse. There is barely room in the bed for her. Often there is an assortment of rawhide chews. Buffy's favorite after-dinner activity is a good hour of rawhide chewing, followed by a nap in Daddy's lap. She still uses our rug occasionally, but does toilet outside as well. She has begun to see that she can control her bodily functions. However, she cannot always wait until we get a coat on, or hook the leash, etc. So we have paper in the kitchen and Buffy is very good about getting her two front paws on the paper.

Buffy takes every day as a gift. Her tail is always up now, her head is high, and I believe her heart is full. She is gentle and loving, and beginning to trust us. She is bright as a penny and learns quickly. She is still stealing dirty socks, sneaking into Caitie's bed and stealing Caitie's toys. She is constantly surrounded by a stack of toys and rawhides. She seems content and the queen of all that she surveys. One night, the cat Patch, began to choke and wheeze. I think he had a hairball. Buffy ran to him and began to lick his throat. Caitie followed her lead. It was touching to watch the two dogs' concern for their cat. Buffy loves everyone and everything. She is exploring life and learning to enjoy it. She has learned a new trick.

Everyday Bob and I drive to the local Quik-Check and buy coffee. We put very thin red straw stirrers in the mugs. Two days ago, I saw the straw fall to the floor. I thought that perhaps it had accidentally gotten tangled in Buffy's beard. Well, yesterday, we got the coffee and we watched as Buffy deftly removed the straw from the coffee mug and chewed it.

It is absolutely an affirmation of the goodness of this animal to watch how she approaches life. My little fox is almost tamed. She is my responsibility forever. I am blessed. Bob is in love with her, and Caitie has become very attached to her. What a gift Buffy is. How lucky we have been to have found her!

As a post script to this story, Ginny added a follow-up before this book went into publication:

It has been a little more than a year since we first received Buffy from the loving arms of Altha. She came to us a terrified creature, quivering, unwilling to make eye contact; shying away from any physical contact. The one bright spot in her eyes was our then nine-month-old wire puppy, Caitie. She immediately adored Caitie and fell in love with our rescue cat, now know as Their cat-Patch. It was with the human kind that she wanted no contact. Buffy was afraid of everything that didn't have four legs—us, the wind, the world.

She had many medical problems, all of which we have been able to deal with. She has diabetes insipidus, which means that she craves inordinate amounts of water, and we must regulate her intake. She has an incredible output of urine, urinating at least ten to sixteen times a day. You can take her out and she will go, only to come back in and pee again. We have come to terms with this. She has learned that she can control, to some extent, her bodily functions. She no longer pees all over the place. She has learned to go outside, and we have papers in a corner of the kitchen for her emergency stops. No worse than an old man with prostate problems.

To date, her teeth have held up. I hope that they continue to do so. Her broken canine has not been extracted. The vet is pleased with the condition of her teeth, relatively speaking.

Initially, Buffy would study everything that Caitie did, and things that we did to Caitie. Her anxiety level was high when we lifted Caitie up. Buffy would become visibly upset. She would inspect Caitie from tip to toe when we put her down.

Little by little, Buffy came to know that human touch was a good thing, a kind, loving caress, something to be enjoyed, not just endured.

Last year, when she was new and visitors came to our home, Buffy would shy away, cringing from their touch. Now, she does her little dance of joy and greets people eye to eye, tail wagging.

Bob and I take Buffy every day to the Quick Chek where we buy coffee and the paper. We started this to try to socialize her to new people. At first, Buffy would sit tensed in Bob's arms, tolerating the ride. Now, Buffy nudges and whines to get Bob and me moving to the car for a ride. She will often bring the stuffed toy favorite of the day or a piece of rawhide along for the ride.

And, she has a Quick Chek fan club! There are regular customers who know her name and her story. They make a point of coming over to the car and petting Buffy, who responds by licking their hands and face, and joyously wiggling and wagging her tail.

She and Caitie have had a few spats; usually, they are started by Caitie, (14lbs) and finished by Buffy (25 lbs). They soon make up and sleep cuddled up in the bed together. Buffy now sleeps in bed with Bob and me and Caitie and Patch. Fortunately, we have a king sized bed which is often covered in toys and rawhide that Buffy brings with her to bed.

When she first arrived, she didn't know how to play. Now, at least once a night, Buffy and Caitie play terrier tears. They both race through the rooms chasing each other. We have a center hall colonial that must have been designed for just this game. There is no greater fun than racing around the rooms in a circle, in hot pursuit, first Caitie chasing Bufffy and then Buffy chasing Caitie. They bounce from couch to couch, on and off the beds. Life is good. They growl and sound as if they are pit bulls locked in deadly combat. Usually, Caitie flies off the couch and over Buffy. On occasion, Buffy lands on Caitie or they bump each other in midair and poor Caitie goes flying. Caitie has taught Buffy how to play with Their-cat-Patch, whom they both idolize. Buffy now assumes the play position and bounces joyously around Patch. Both wires feel it is their duty to clean his ears.
 Buffy is brilliant. I believe she is the smartest of all the six wires that I have had the pleasure to share my home and heart with. She loves her life. She is particularly fond of mealtimes and literally sings for her supper. She chortles, she trills, she yodels.

What a symphony!

When I first took Buffy, I thought that I had a lot to give her and that she would benefit from being in our home. I did not realize that she was the gift to us. It has been an incredibly humbling experience to share our lives with her. We were patient, and every day she came a little closer to our hearts. It is wonderful how our hearts are expandable. There is always room for one more of these wonderful creatures. I carry within my heart all the wires of my life. It is reassuring to know that they are always within my grasp.

I have always played a game of "I should have named you." Buffy came to us with her name. We did not want confuse her by changing it since she really knew it. Often, I have found that rescues come to me with a name that they do not know. I find that particularly sad because they have lost even that small part of their identity.

Well, I dubbed Buffy, Buffy Marie, because she reminded me of my Aunt Marie. She was stocky, big-boned, the eldest of seven sisters, and quite a presence. But, playing the name game with Buffy I came to realize that had I not known her name, I would have named her Rose. She has truly blossomed like a rose. Buffy is our Rose, she has grown in love, watered in kindness, and blossomed in trust. She is our gift. She has taught us what resilience is, how kindness causes one to flourish. Every day, we see a new petal open on our rosebud. Her scent is sweet, the aroma of love. Her roots are deepening in our hearts and she is turning her face toward the sun.

The only thorns that tear our hearts are the remnants of her old place—she still cringes if one approaches her too quickly, or makes a sudden movement toward her head.

It is the thorn that reminds us of the growth, and that one must handle a rose gently.

Author's Bio: Ginny Mastondrea lives in New Jersey with her husband, Bob, the dogs Buffy and Catie and Their-cat-Patch. Semi-retired, she worked for 35 years for the NJ Division of Youth and Family Services in protective services. A licensed clinical social worker, she now works part-time doing adoptee search and reunification counseling. She devotes her spare time to Fox Terrier Rescue for smooth and wire fox terriers. She is contemplating writing two novels—a children's book about Caitie and the kink in her tail, and another about a young Irish-American girl growing up in the late 50's-early 60's in a big city and becoming a child welfare worker

DIANE CLOVER-EVANS

BUMPER, CANINE THERAPIST

By Diane Clover-Evans

My mother developed heart irregularities about a year ago. Now she was in the hospital once again with chest pains. I found her propped up on a pillow while Pop sat in a straight chair beside her bed.

Ma's hospital room had all the charm of a funeral home. The shades were drawn shut, permitting only a bit of light into the room. Everything was quiet, almost like a tomb. She had lost considerable weight and looked extremely pale, but as always, Ma smiled and put on a brave face for me.

"Hey, Ma. What 'cha doing here? Don't you have something better to do?"

"I'd love to go home to my garden. This place is so depressing."

Tubes sprouted from her arms and electrode wires snaked from her chest to various monitors that beeped, blinked or hummed. I noticed that her blood pressure hovered in the highest range.

"No wonder about that, Ma." I fluffed the pillows and took a good look at Pop. There he sat, leaning over the end of the bed, looking forlorn and lost.

"Hey, Pop. I almost didn't see you over there in the dark. Let's open these shades and let the sunshine in."

Pop jumped up, grabbed me by the arm and pulled me out into the hallway. "Don't you come in here and disturb her. She needs things as quiet as possible. I'm afraid she won't be with us much longer."

"Now Pop, I'm a nurse. I know something about these things. Keeping her in a dark room isn't the ticket. She needs everything to be cheerful and upbeat. This doom and gloom attitude of yours is only increasing her stress, and that increases her blood pressure. So lighten up."

Our conversation went nowhere. Pop was determined to protect Ma even if it killed her. Arguing was a waste of time, and I had to do something. I peeked into her room and winked at her. "Lady, I'm coming back with a little surprise for you. Just hang in there."

The big smile on her face was a reward in itself.

I'm a surgical nurse. My job requires working under extreme pressure. Due to the stress, I've developed an ulcer, and now my stomach rules my life. When a friend recommended that a pet might help me cope with stress, I found an adorable black puppy with a lovable whiskery face. I called him "Bumper."

Just seeing this guy every day made me smile and he'd smile right back at me with his head tipped to one side, his tongue lolling from his mouth, his whiskers twitching, and his ears cocked forward. Even a thought of him during the day made me smile. As an added bonus, my stomach didn't bother me nearly as much since the arrival of Bumper.

Ma always enjoyed playing with my dog, and she really needed him now. I decided to somehow take Bumper to the hospital to visit her. No matter what Pop said, Ma needed a sense of fun and enjoyment. It was virtually a matter of life and death.

Getting Bumper up to her hospital room would be a trick. The dog was so large that he took up the entire extended cab area of my F150 truck. He'd certainly be noticed if we walked casually in to the hospital entrance. That just wouldn't do. Best to do this after dark and find another way up to Ma's room, I thought. I drove to the far side of the hospital parking lot and left Bumper in the truck while I performed a reconnaissance mission. Dressed in my surgical greens, I walked into the service entrance as if I owned the place and then wandered around looking for ideas. Aha! The laundry room! I slipped in and found a large laundry cart. After stuffing in some sheets and towels, I rolled it out to my truck. Getting Bumper in the cart was not going to be easy. He sniffed at the cart, then backed off, cocked his head sideways and looked at me.

"OK, Bumper, I gotta get you in this cart." I lifted his front-quarters into the cart so that front half of him was inside and his rear dangled over the edge. He whimpered and struggled a bit but I managed to heave his rear quarters into the cart. Bumper sat down in the cart and cocked his head again, giving me that "What the heck are you doing?" look.

I checked, and there was no one else in the parking lot so the coast was clear.

"OK, Bump. Here we go." I unfolded the sheets and towels and threw them over Bumper's head. He stuck his nose out and his whiskers twitched.

Back again at the service door, I found another problem. The threshold had a raised ridge and I had to get the 100 pounds of puppy and laundry cart over that barrier. It didn't look like a problem on the first try, but the cart almost overturned, and Bumper grumbled when it hit hard against the ridge.

"It's OK, Bump. Just hang tight and I'll get you over it." I backed up and ran at the threshold. The cart hit the ridge and bounced back hard. The laundry raised up and looked me in the eye with whiskers twitching.

"Hey, settle down. I'll figure out something."

"Hrrrrump." The laundry sighed and crumpled back down in the cart. I tried once more but Bumper shifted his weight and tipped the cart over and jumped out. Trailing a sheet and a towel, he raced out into the parking lot.

"Bumper, you get your black butt back here right now!"

From behind, I heard a voice. "But you didn't ask very nicely."

I turned around to see an elderly janitor smiling broadly at me. I could have just died on the spot.

"Oh, I'm so sorry. I'm trying to get my dog to come back here. He's out there sitting by the truck."

"Young lady, that is one huge dog. Why are you trying to smuggle him into the hospital? Don't you know that's against the rules?"

I explained the situation to him as we walked out to the truck, picking up a sheet and the towel in route.

Bumper waited with his tail beating the pavement and his whiskers twitching. A true gentleman, Bumper smiled and raised his paw to the man, who smiled and shook it.

"Obviously you need some help." Before I could reply, he petted Bumper and helped him back into the cart. We hid Bumper under the laundry and wheeled the cart back to the service entrance. Between the two of us, we got it over the threshold barrier.

"Thank you. Thanks so much."

"No problem. You've got a mighty heavy load there," he replied. "The service elevator is right over there. One thing, if you get caught, please don't mention that I aided and abetted you in this subversive activity." Then he smiled at Bumper and returned to his work.

The rest of the plan went along fairly easily. I took the service elevator up to the 4th floor and came out directly across from Ma's room. It was still dim in there, lit only by a night light. Dad was snoring in his chair, but Ma was awake.

"Got ya a surprise, Ma," I whispered. I pulled off the laundry and Bumper's hairy snout poked out with the twitching whiskers.

"Oh, your puppy!" Ma squealed.

That woke up Pa. "I just can't believe you did this. You broke the hospital rules. They'll make us leave. Get that dog outa here."

"No, I want to see Bumper," Ma insisted, "Now just shut up and go back to sleep."

"Calm down, Pa. Help me get Bumper out of the cart."

That turned out to be much easier than getting Bumper into the cart. Bumper trotted over to Ma and snuggled his nose under her hand. She patted his head and baby-talked while he twitched his whiskers and wagged his stub tail. He sniffed her IV and then slimed her hand. She laughed softly. Then Bumper rested his head on her arm, twitched his whiskers, let out a big sigh and wagged his entire butt. Ma was laughing.

I glanced at the blood pressure monitor and found that the reading was falling. When I pointed this out to Pop, he relaxed a bit and shut the door. A few jokes and several Bumper stories later, I saw they were both enjoying their canine visitor. Later we heard a nurse walking down the hallway. I pushed Bumper under the bed and told him to lie down and be quiet. While we held our breath, she came in and checked the monitors and wrote notes on Ma's chart.

As she left the room, the nurse looked at us over her shoulder and said, "Nice puppy." Pop let out his breath and Bumper peeped out from under the bed. I could only see one eye and his whiskery snout but we all heard the "thump-thump-thump."

"What is that?" Pop asked.

"That's his tail pounding on the underside of my bed," Ma explained. "Missy, you have a really special puppy!" Bumper crawled out and wiggled his butt. Before the doctor came in for his evening rounds, I sequestered Bumper under the bed once again. The doctor looked around the room, opened the closet and asked, "Where is the puppy?"

My heart sank. I just knew he was going throw us out of the hospital. Bumper crawled out, sat down, twitched his whiskers and raised his paw to the doctor.

"Doctor, this is Bumper. Please don't make him leave," Ma said.

"Yes, he's had my wife laughing all evening. He's been good for her," Pop chimed in.

"Look at the blood pressure reading," I added.

"Hmmm. I see that the blood pressure is falling." He checked Ma's chart. "Well, the blood pressure is the lowest it's been in days."

"Please, may I bring him back to see her?" I asked.

The doctor picked up Ma's chart and began to write. Then he smiled and said, "I expect to see Bumper in here every day until your mother is dismissed." He left the room and then stopped and stuck his head back in the door. "By the way, you can use the front door. We don't have many laundry carts to spare."

After he left, I picked up the chart and read, "Canine therapist, Bumper, is allowed daily visits as needed for therapy treatment."

Author's Bio: Diane Clover-Evans holds degrees from Vanderbilt University and the Georgia Institute of Technology. "In my 'real job' I am a Civil engineer and have had several papers published in various professional journals. However I love to write fiction. I've studied creative writing with the Institute of Children's Literature and the Long Ridge Writers Group." Presently Diane lives in Georgia with her husband, Tom, their Bouvier Des Flandres dog, T Rex, a rat called Pinky and a cockatiel named T-Bird but more often called "Screachure Creature." Her e-mail address is dcevans@suite101.com.

CLYDE'S GIFT
A BRIEF RESURRECTION

By Tova Gabrielle

When folks in Massachusetts' Pioneer Valley used to see me strolling down Pleasant Street with a white bird perched happily on my right shoulder, they would do double takes or stop.

Clyde the female cockatoo would raise her crest, fluff out her feathers, and give a light-hearted, "Hi Clyde!" and they would laugh, look surprised or say "Hi Clyde!" back.

But then the frequently-asked questions would inevitably start up. When faced with the conundrum of what to say to a human donning a bird.... or, what to say to a bird with a human underfoot, people seem to be at a loss after the introduction.

"Is that your bird?"

"No, I'm her human," I'd say.

"Can she think?" "Does she feel?"

"I don't know, why don't you ask her?" (kinder than, "Can *you*?")

"Is that bird real?"

Deadpan, "NO" (Not, at least, "Are YOU?")

OK; so maybe you have to be pet-codependent, like me, to understand why I would get uppity about an animal.

For one thing, I can attest to the new findings that parrots understand and use language appropriately. And they are extraordinarily attuned to their environment and the feelings of people and animals around them. For another thing, I didn't want Clyde to be any more bothered than she'd been during her former life behind bars: before I'd rescued her, she'd done 20 years for the crime of being wild. I didn't, however, realize what I was in for. Once Clyde burst into my life, she began a cute but devastating take-over. Yet I simply couldn't pass her on to someone

59

who would again abandon her. So, being both smitten and anxious, like anyone newly involved, I opted for the well-worn path of denial.

Clyde played her part in this dysfunctional relationship. As "Frog Princess", she demanded (and was granted) a seat by my plate and an occasional spot beneath my bed-covers.

And, like most couples, we began having problems—particularly when I refused certain aspects of her affections.

First offense involved my rejecting her efforts to feed me. In avian social morays, regurgitating into your beloved's mouth is a high honor. Not only is this a form of foreplay, but the method used by mother birds to feed their bappies in the nest. There was another problem, as well: Clyde wanted to mate, and preferably, with a human; male if possible, but she'd take what she could get. (Having bonded with humans when she first opened her eyes and saw one, she was doomed to identify with, and lust after that object henceforth.) Poor Clyde. She never hesitated to assume the prone position with complete strangers, especially all males. And once on her back, she always made sure to lift a wing, so her breast would be accessible for scratching.

Besides being a hopeless romantic Clyde was an gregarious entertainer. Once, Gary, an actor friend who Clyde sometimes let me "borrow", included her in a comic rendition of Elton John's, "Crocodile Rock." For "Cockatoo Rock," Gary dressed in feather boas and danced as he sang. Clyde perched on his shoulder and strutted, talked and turned in accordance.

When the act ended, Clyde proceeded to bar-hop—bounding up and down the counter and onto the welcoming shoulders of the line of people seated there, punctuating each pounce with a victorious little squawk.

Overall, Clyde was a hit—although some people nearly spilled their drinks. However, there is always someone who is afraid of wild winged beings, be they angels or birds (and as far as I'm concerned, there is not much difference). And when such a soul cried out drunkenly, "Oh no, a bird!" I just couldn't resist cracking, "It's OK, I can protect her from you!"

Of course, my attitude didn't set a good example to Clyde, who always tried to insure that people knew she was an insider. If ignored, she'd fly to the highest place possible, puff out her chest, spread her wings widely, and let out a screech that was meant to travel a mile in her native Australian rainforest. "I am Queen and if you don't show reverence, I'll have you for dinner!"

My mother, who eventually stopped visiting, wouldn't cow-tow, but would cover her ears, wince, and complain, "She's so RUDE!" Most visitors didn't usually return to my home. Nor did they care, when I'd explain miserably that Clyde simply wanted to be included. They didn't feel guilty when I'd point out that they'd failed to return her greeting of "Hi Clyde". They didn't repent after learning that my "child" was as needing and deserving of love as any developing, two-year-old. (However, parrots stay 'two' for as much as 80 long years. Of course I left that tidbit out.)

They turned to stone when I tried explaining that she didn't know that screaming didn't endear people to her.

As people became scarce in my life, I thanked Clyde for helping me to sort out who my "real" friends were, and continued accommodating and denying. How could I overlook that my child was a genius? Clyde, along with her sidekick, Timmy the male Goffins Cockatoo, learned to go into and stay in the trees behind my house, and to fly in for dinner and warmth at night.

When I would be gone, Timmy became an expert at picking locks. He would escape the aviary and proceed on his mission of freeing Clyde. (Goffins are known to become dangerously aggressive if caged together; although, in wider expanses, they will get along fine, as Clyde and Timmy did in the trees.) I stopped putting Clyde in the aviary when I observed that she would approach Timmy sexually and then, when he'd reject her, she would (somewhat understandably) try killing him.

I'd return home to find dishes knocked over, flowers eaten, and banisters chewed. That was when I began whispering to my family about selling her. Whispering because, when I spoke of such horrors, Clyde turned her back and ignored me for awhile.

Ultimately, Clyde bypassed reasoning and got to my heart. From turning summersaults on her stand, to perching on my head and combing my hair with her beak, she tried her best to help. Her favorite favor was helping sort laundry, especially socks: jumping into my drawers and throwing them on the floor.

Well, I guess a supernatural bird like Clyde couldn't go on like that forever, nor could I....

A breeder had warned me long ago that when you work with birds you are working with wild animals. Unlike cats and dogs, they are not acclimated to domesticity.

He said, "sooner or later, you're going to lose one."

We'd only been working with birds for two decades at most.

"You just can't anticipate all the things that can go wrong."

Tragically, the breeder's words were to come true....

Clyde, who got into everything, died from a freak household accident when a vase fell on her in the confusion of moving. Yet, even at death's door she communicated a boundless affection:

After her vital functions had apparently quit, I'd wrapped her in my dark green wool poncho and carried her out to the woods behind my house. I placed her gently on the ground, with wings spread and head down, covering her lightly with leaves so I could spot her. I'd return when my grief subsided, along with my partner Jim, and give her a proper burial.

An hour or two later, Jim and I donned a flashlight and climbed the pine needle laden hill on which she lay, but we could not find her. We were calling to her, saying "Clyde, we love you, Clyde we are sorry," when I finally spotted the white of her tail. I yelled to Jim, "Over here!"

We no sooner got there when, to our astonishment, she lifted her head.

"My God, She's alive!" I called out, quickly scooping her up.

We frantically called information to find a vet and discovered an animal hospital that was open all night. It was an hour away.

The vet told us that she would, most likely, die within hours. I looked down into her face and thought, oddly, of a lion. In a last ditch effort, he gave her an injection of steroids to reduce the swelling in her head. At our insistence, he returned her to us, warning us that birds can't be expected to survive head traumas. Jim and I sensed that if anything was keeping her alive it was our connection with her. Like a string our mutual affection seemed to be tugging her in, as if she were a kite, being pulled against winds imminent death.

Birds are ingenious at "keeping things light". Back home, in my bedroom, she had an indescribably serene "smile" on her face, as she lay, breathing shallowly, upon my chest.

"Clyde we love you! What a bird! Stay with us! You can do it!" we begged. That night, lamentably, there were to be no ardent protests; only acquiescent grunts when we were naming Clyde's closest people. When I named Gary, she grunted louder. And at the mention of my son, I could feel her heartbeat increase and felt a slight shiver pass through her. All night, she lay on my chest with a blissful look that transcended all physical constraints.

Her good nature emanated through her breathing and a deep peace filled the room as she rested, sometimes with eyes semi-open and other times closed. We were begging her to stay with it, not to go, when it hit me that perhaps it was selfish to wish this on her. What did she want?

It is a fact that when a storm is approaching, eagles will sense it and perch on the highest branches they can find. There, they allow increasing winds to help lift them high above the dark clouds. They soar above the storm, returning to Earth only after it passes.

As the dark clouds of our grief had gathered, Clyde seemed to be patiently waiting out our storm in a transcendent state that soothed our resistance to her final flight.

During that night we reasoned: Clearly, she could not remain in that twisted body. Wasn't it enough to have these last hours together with her? She seemed to be gliding into some invisible expansion of space.

Sensing her gentle rapture, we felt blessed, and finally even resolved. During the night, our dread had changed to acceptance.

At 7 A.M. I opened my eyes to see Clyde lifting her head from my chest, opening both eyes wide, and looking right at me.

I thought, "My God, she's recovered!" as she flapped her wings once, hard. And then—just as suddenly—her body stiffened.

What remained was no longer beautiful. Her mouth was open and I could see blood. I turned to Jim to tell him she had just died but he was not listening—not to me, anyway.

Instead he was having a vision of Clyde: having flown out of her lifeless body with that one final flap of her wings, she took off like a shot. Then, returning briefly, he watched as she joyously circled our heads, before taking off for good.

Author's Bio: Tova Gabrielle has published non-fiction, poetry, and memoirs in *The Phoenix; Twins Magazine; Moxie; Newtopia; Divorce Magazine; Hebrew Immigrant Aid Society's 120 Stories; Two River View,* and *Big Bridge,* amongst others. She is presently pursuing ceramics. "It seems I'm best employed as a shaman, but I can't find a job opening. I am certain that I was not born to increase the gross national product." She retired early from being a Psychotherapist/ Substance Abuse Counselor.

CONFESSIONS FROM A VET'S OFFICE

By Avis Townsend

My vet office is an upscale facility, not cheap, and I was sure clients who came in with their pets would be responsible, loving, and eager to see their animals have the best of care. Well, it was the first of many shocks I received while working there.

Yes, it's upscale, but that doesn't stop people from being stupid when it comes to pets, and within a year, I had seen all ends of the care spectrum.

On the caring-too-much scale, there were ladies who were actually killing their pets with kindness. One elderly woman, who had recently acquired a Pomeranian, visited the office once a month with some canine malady or the other...*the dog is constipated, the dog has diarrhea, the dog can't pee, the dog is peeing all over the place.* She fretted so much we were afraid she'd kill the dog with her home remedies. She gave the dog a baby enema, then Kaopectate to stop the runs. Then she wanted penicillin for an imagined cold. Then she needed grooming to take out imaginary hairballs. Finally, after a few months, she settled down and let her dog be a dog, and everyone was able to relax.

Now she only calls once a month or so, fretting about some imaginary ailment, but generally the techs can calm her fears.

Ladies with elderly cats will go to great lengths to keep them alive. Sometimes it's good, but at other times they'd be better off letting them go. Fluid injections are the biggest thing. As cats age, they seem to lose a lot of water, sometimes to diabetes, sometimes because—well, they're old—and their owners don't want to let go. One lady brought her cat in three times a week for six months, having the cat injected so it could hydrate. Its hair had fallen out, and it hardly resembled a cat anymore, being twenty years old. It had a good life on this earth and it was time to go on to the next life, but the owner wouldn't have it. She insisted—either our doctors do it or she'd go elsewhere. Eventually, the poor thing died in its sleep. However, another lady with an eighteen-year-old diabetic cat also brought it in for fluids, eventually learning how to do it herself. In her case, the cat thrived, and is still thriving, working toward its twentieth year.

It was nice to see these type of caring individuals bringing in their pets, and this was what I'd expected when I began to work there. However, there is a down side, a black side, and it's a real eye-opener.

For instance, did you know that spring is maggot season? It's very common for people who keep rabbits in hutches outside to come in because the rabbit is chewing on its behind, and we know before the owners arrive that we will have to shave the bunny's bum and remove maggots that are crawling in and out of its rectum. People don't realize that flies are attracted to moist, smelly areas, and rabbit hutches not cleaned frequently are a fly magnet. When they hatch their eggs (maggots), the larva feed on the blood of the animal in the cage.

But there is also a maggot season for dogs. Several people dropped by with long-haired outdoor dogs because their animals wouldn't stop digging themselves. One of these dogs sticks in my memory because the dog was very kind and its owner was very rich, and in the medical profession no less. The dog, a chow, was brought in for grooming. When the groomer shaved it, she found holes all over its body, holes filled with maggots. We were shocked the dog was still alive, and it was very anemic from the blood loss. We called the owner to explain the situation, and she laughed and said she'd never heard of such a thing. She didn't seem concerned at all, finding the whole incident a big joke.

We kept the dog for several days, medicating it, dressing its wounds, and the owner took it home after paying a large bill. The following winter, the owner's husband called to tell us the dog was outside, lying on its side, trying to die. "He doesn't seem to be in much pain, so we're just going to let death ride itself out. We only called so you could take our name out of your files." Thoughtful, weren't they?

Then there was the guinea pig lady. She said, "I came home and found his foot bleeding all over." She'd carried him into the office wrapped in a towel, which was saturated with blood.

Upon examination, the doctor found toenails so long they curled around into the guinea pig's feet, and a foot sore so old it had turned to gangrene. The guinea pig was so skinny it was malnourished. It died on the table while it was being examined. The owner sobbed and sobbed.

Then she came to the front desk, saying she couldn't pay the bill right away because she had just spent $1,000 on a golden retriever, and as soon as she built her money back up she'd be bringing that in for shots. She eventually paid her bill, but we never saw the retriever.

Next comes euthanasia season, generally around the first of December. Owners of older, sick, and crippled animals decide Christmas time is the time to get rid of these pets, because they're planning Christmas parties and they don't want the animals ruining the happy theme. So, they bring them in and have them put down, discarding them like the garbage.

Once a cat owner called to have his cat put to sleep. Why? Because it had become boring It seems the cat was fun as a kitten, running around, climbing the curtains, and getting into things. But now he was grown up, and just sat around, cleaning himself. They wanted to get rid of him and get another kitten. It was a wonderful cat, and one of the doctors talked them into letting her take it, rather than killing it because it was boring.

I found the euthansias emotionally draining. Someone told me I'd get used to it, but I never did. I have gone home several nights in tears, and have seen ignorance and stupidity of many pet owners.

I should have resigned my first week on the job. I was told a euthanasia was coming in, and I was not prepared for this big burly guy coming through the door, holding a beautiful long-haired calico cat. His wife had called earlier in the day and said the cat was full of cancer and had to be put down. Most of the time, people brought their animals in carriers, or dogs on leashes under the counter, so I wouldn't be able to see them. But this time the man walked in holding his sweet calico cat.

He told me to come over and look at her stomach. A huge tumor, which looked like a sea anemone, was growing out of it. The vet said it was a mammary tumor, very common in female cats who have litter after litter, are unspayed, or who are spayed after six litters of kittens. The cancer had metastasized through her little body.

The vet techs escorted the man and his kitty into the treatment room, giving him one last moment to be with his cat before she was put out of her misery. When it was over, they left him to say his goodbyes. We waited and waited, but he didn't come out. Finally, after an hour the techs went in to check on him and he was sobbing like a baby—this huge, burly guy with a flannel shirt and beard looked more like a tough guy biker than anything else. He was petting his cat and sobbing. Finally, he came out and handed me a blank check to fill out because he couldn't write through tears and sadness.

Then he said, "I'm happy knowing she's with my mother now."

I replied, "and someday you'll all be together again." I don't know how I held it together there, but I cried all the way home.

I learned a lot at my job. Things I thought were commonplace turned into big no-no's at home. The bone situation is one of them. I know not to give my animals chicken or turkey bones, because they can splinter and puncture their stomachs, intestines, or anyplace between going down and coming out. But I'd always given them ham bones and pork chop bones. I don't anymore.

One day a woman called the office, crying hysterically. She went out in the back yard to find her Rottweiler dead, foam all over its mouth and paws. "I just gave it a pork chop about a half hour before, do you think he choked?"

I asked the vet, telling her about the symptoms but not telling her about the pork chop. Without stopping to have to think about it she said, "Foaming at the mouth? He choked on something."

When I told the girl her dog had choked, she became inconsolable. She was tortured because she killed her own dog.

Another man brought his dog in because it hadn't defecated in three days. It kept trying, but it just couldn't go to the bathroom. X-rays showed a large mass at the end of the intestine. Fortunately, surgery wasn't needed, but it took three days of barium enemas and probing to remove chards of a ham bone that accumulated at the base of the rectum and refused to pass.

I used to give my dogs pork chop bones all the time when I ate pork. Who'd have thought they could choke to death? I let them eat ham bones also. I thought I was doing them a big favor. Who knew I could be slowly killing them?

Then there is the subject of breeders. Except for puppy millers, most dog breeders care about their animals. But some breed for perfection, and want nothing to do with selling a "pet quality" dog, one that will be a great dog, but might be the wrong color, have an ear that's a little too long, or a strange-shaped nose. Most breeders sell these "seconds" as pet quality, and stipulate on their pedigree papers that they cannot be bred or shown.

But some breeders just want to be rid of these dogs, and they will kill them or set them aside to die. We saw this first-hand in two different episodes.

The first involved a tiny Shi-Tzu puppy, no more than four weeks old. A woman brought this puppy in, half dead. Her neighbor, a breeder, had sat it aside away from the rest of the litter, waiting for it to die. It wasn't the right color, she explained. The woman's daughter was babysitting at the puppy house and saw it in a box, and asked if she could take it. The girl was devastated, wondering how humans could just let such a tiny thing die.

Also, the breeder had said it was a female, but upon vet inspection we found out it was a male. He was very cute—black and white, all curls. The doctor gave him fluid under the skin and the new owner called the next day and said he started walking around. The vet told her she still had a long way to go, as the puppy was left quite a while without nourishment. With love and care from his new owners, however, he lived, and he is now a happy, healthy adult.

We had another breeder in for a caesarian on a Bassett hound. As the puppies were delivered, the owner examined each one carefully, making sure they were okay. One of the puppies had something wrong, a cleft palate or something major, and the owners wanted to destroy it. They stuffed it in a plastic bag and zipped it up, hoping it would suffocate. One of the vet techs said she would euthanize it, but the owners refused, not wanting to pay any additional charges for a puppy that would net them no profit. After fifteen minutes the puppy was still alive, so the vet tech took it from the bag and euthanized it anyway. The breeders were furious, and said they wouldn't pay. She said she paid for it herself, "because we don't believe in suffering here."

Another woman brought in a cat last week, a stray who seemed sick. She spent $514 trying to get him to live, but he died. Liver damage was the final diagnosis. They think he might have got into anti freeze. Antifreeze is very dangerous to pets. It is almost certain death to cats. A few drops can kill them, and it's a very painful death. If your pet gets into it, call the vet immediately. There is an anecdote, and it's vodka. If you can't get hold of a vet, force feed vodka immediately, as it dilutes the poisonous effects of the anti-freeze. However, to do the best job, the vodka must be given intravenously, and it works better in dogs than in cats. Generally, if a cat drinks anti-freeze it will die shortly.

So remember to keep all antifreeze in a tight container, and don't park leaking vehicles on cement, or there could be heartbreaking results. Antifreeze has a sweet taste and actually beckons pets to try it. Once it's in their system, the damage begins immediately.

Another danger to dogs is cat litter. For some reason, dogs enjoy chewing on the contents of the cat box, and as they do this, litter gets into their stomachs. Clumping litter can get harder and harder, and clumps will gather together and not be dissolved. We had a dog who ate so much it had formed a large block inside the stomach. The doctors tried diluting it with barium, but nothing worked. The owners could not afford surgery to get it out, so they took the dog home, hoping the litter eventually would break up and come out naturally. It didn't. The dog died a month later, another painful, dragged-out death.

My dogs have helped themselves to the litter box many times, and though I thought it was disgusting, I never realized it could be fatal. So, now all cat boxes are off limits to my dogs, either put up or locked away where they can't get at them.

Veterinarian visits can be very expensive, but our pets are worth it. Also, if we skimp now we could really pay later. Distemper/parvo shots are relatively inexpensive. Trying to cure the disease can cost hundreds of times more. Routine blood work prior to surgery (spays, neuters, dentistry's) is an expense some people choose to do without.

"The animal's young," they say, "what can go wrong?"

I have seen cats die on the table as soon as anesthetic is administered, or dogs suffering permanent brain damage from dying on the table and being brought back. The blood work tells if there could be problems. It averages $25 to $30. Complications could cost hundreds of dollars, or eventual death if it survives the initial attack. Which would you prefer?

If your pet is healthy, you'll still spend around $100 a year for a physical, wormer, and needed shots. That's less than $9 a month to spend on someone who shows you unconditional love. How much love are you willing to show your pet?

DONKEY SERENADE

By Alan Campbell

A girl in my neighborhood in Cape Town, South Africa, owned a donkey named Andy. Andy had his own enclosure and we kids used to pat him over the fence, and feed him grass. One day his owner - I think her name was Anne - came out and spoke to us. She said she would be grateful if we would gather grass for Andy whenever we came around, and then asked if we would like to take him for a ride. Of course we delightedly agreed, and she allowed us to ride him up and down the grassed sidewalk beside her house.

To us this was the nearest thing we would ever get to the universal kids' dream of a pony, and we gathered grass with glee and visited Andy and Anne regularly. Soon we won Anne's confidence, and she would on occasions allow us to take Andy away for a whole day. We would go back to our own neighborhood and Andy was the center of attention for wonderful hours of fun.

Then came the impending church bazaar and I had this wonderful idea! If Anne would consent to let me borrow Andy I could give donkey rides a ticket a time, and raise money for church funds. There was also to be a 'fancy dress' competition at the bazaar, and I further reasoned that if I dressed in my cowboy outfit and rode Andy, the judges would surely have to give me a prize.

To my delight, Anne agreed, and on the day I collected Andy. Anne had prepared him well. He was completely rigged out with saddle and reins and all the trappings, and I felt as proud as punch as I led him into the church grounds, resplendent in my cowboy outfit, and feeling ten feet tall.

It was still early, and people were bustling around setting up stalls and preparing for the public onslaught to come. I led Andy over to a grassy spot where I knew he would be happy to graze and left him free to browse. He was a happy little donkey, and by now I knew him to be perfectly behaved.

Then the man with the loud speaker system decided to try out his set-up with some music. Unfortunately, he started with the volume control turned right up, and this sudden cacophony of sound erupted through the high mounted speakers with alarming impact. It startled everyone - but Andy's reaction was to bolt. Obviously frightened by this noise, he started to kick up his heels and run in every direction. People screamed as he charged by them, and I sprinted after him to try and bring him in check. He rounded the church building ahead of me and entered the open hall doors at a full gallop.

I winced as I heard women screaming and trestle tables crashing to the wooden floor as Andy unleashed his path of havoc across the church hall. I ran after him, but he turned and made his way back out again before I could get to his reins. Women screamed and scattered again as he made his thunderous exit, hooves clumping loudly over the wooden floor. Once outside he changed direction and headed for the main gate, which was standing open.

My blood froze because the road he was heading for was a busy thoroughfare, and I feared that in his blind panic he would run straight out into the traffic and be struck by a car. I also knew that even if he survived the traffic, there was another horror to contemplate. Andy knew his way home! This I had discovered on the many occasions I had taken him home from an outing. There was no need to guide him, as he would trot along and instinctively take all the right roads home. Imagine Anne's displeasure if Andy were to arrive home in that state without me. I could never look her in the face again, and worse still, she would never allow me to take Andy out ever again.

All these things raced through my mind as Andy raced for the gate, and I knew that I had no hope whatever of catching up with him. Despair overtook me and I knew the frustration of total helplessness.

Then, out of the corner of my eye, I saw my elder brother, Neville, sprinting like fury across the grounds ahead of us, intent on heading Andy off at the gate. They reached the opening together, and Neville launched himself through the air in a desperate dive that got one of his arms around Andy's neck. He hung on tenaciously as Andy bucked and kicked and tried everything to dislodge him. But Neville's weight had slowed him and turned his head, so that he was steered onto the sidewalk outside the gate and not into the traffic. By then I had caught up with them, and together we dragged the reluctant Andy back into the church grounds and managed to calm him down.

I was hesitant to continue with the donkey rides after that performance of skittishness, but my fears were unfounded, and once Andy had calmed down again, he performed like a gentleman, and was definitely the star of the day.

I personally avoided going into the hall where the ladies had been scared silly earlier on, and the day turned brighter when I was awarded a prize for "the most original turnout" at the fancy dress competition!

Author's Bio: Alan Campbell was born in Cape Town, South Africa. After 47 years of working as a soil and rock technician, he has now retired. Over the years he has written numerous plays for radio, but his specialties are poetry, as well as fiction and nonfiction short stories. Alan and his wife now reside in Pretoria, South Africa. He works part-time, and is continuing with his love of writing.

FAMILY DOG

Author unknown

The family's dog was bought to guard,
Chained to a post in a chilly backyard,
Housed in a shed that was airless and dark,
And every few weeks had a run in the park.

When boredom set in with no fun and no work,
One day it broke loose and went quietly berserk,
Pa couldn't fathom just why it went wild,
As it flattened his wife and then bit his child.

The police were called in to sort out the mess,
And the whole sorry tale was revealed in the press,
The Rescue Society was really annoyed,
So, the dog was re-homed, and the owners destroyed.

FRIENDS FOREVER

Author Unknown

A man and his dog were walking along a road. The man was enjoying the scenery, when it suddenly occurred to him that he was dead. He remembered dying, and that the dog walking beside him had been dead for years. He wondered where the road was leading them.

After a while, they came to a high, white stone wall along one side of the road. It looked like fine marble. At the top of a long hill, it was broken by a tall arch that glowed in the sunlight. When he was standing before it he saw a magnificent gate in the arch that looked like Mother of Pearl, and the street that led to the gate looked like pure gold. He and the dog walked toward the gate, and as he got closer, he saw man at a desk to one side.

When he was close enough, he called out, "Excuse me, where are we?"

"This is Heaven, sir," the man answered.

"Wow! Would you happen to have some water?" the man asked.

"Of course, sir. Come right in, and I'll have some ice water brought right up." The man gestured, and the gate began to open.

"Can my friend come in, too?" the traveler asked, gesturing toward his dog.

"I'm sorry, sir, but we don't accept pets."

The man thought a moment and then turned back toward the road and continued the way he had been going with his dog.

After another long walk, and at the top of another long hill, he came to a dirt road which led through a farm gate that looked as if it had never been closed. There was no fence.

As he approached the gate, he saw a man inside, leaning against a tree and reading a book.

"Excuse me!" he called to the reader. "Do you have any water?"

"Yeah, sure, there's a pump over there". The man pointed to a place that couldn't be seen from outside the gate. "Come on in."

"How about my friend here?" the traveler gestured to the dog.

"There should be a bowl by the pump."

They went through the gate, and sure enough, there was an old fashioned hand pump with a bowl beside it. The traveler filled the bowl and took a long drink himself, then he gave some to the dog.

When they were full, he and the dog walked back toward the man who was standing by the tree waiting for them

What do you call this place?" the traveler asked.

"This is Heaven," he answered.

"Well, that's confusing," the traveler said. "The man down the road said that was Heaven, too."

"Oh, you mean the place with the gold street and pearly gates? Nope. That's Hell."

"Doesn't it make you mad for them to use your name like that?"

"No. I can see how you might think so, but we're just happy that they screen out the folks who'll leave their best friends behind."

GENTLE NUDGES

By Avis Townsend

The mustangs arrived at our local adoption center from the Bureau of Land Management's Lewisbury, Pennsylvania, holding area about three in the morning. When I got there at eight there were no other humans around—only scared, snorting beasts inside of large, circular pens. Some had their heads down and ears to the side, a sign that they are depressed. Some were defiant, pawing the ground, nostrils flaring, daring me to get close. Being the only human in a barn filled with three hundred wild horses was an awesome experience.

Looking around, I couldn't help but notice one set of ears pricked high, pointed my way. As I moved through the maze of enclosures, they never veered away but remained aimed at me. When I finally approached those ears, a red mare the color of brandy stared at me with interested eyes. When I talked to her she didn't back away but stood in place, watching me intently. There was no fear, no animosity— only interest. Our eyes met, and I couldn't turn away. I felt myself connect with her, and I extended my hand. Other horses sharing the enclosure inched backward, bunched toward the farthest point away from me, but the red horse stood her ground. She stretched out her nose, almost touching my fingertips.

Voices behind me disturbed our connection, and the red horse joined the others at the back of the pen. I walked over to my human counterparts but constantly looked back at the little red mare who had grabbed my soul.

The man in charge informed me that eighty people had already mailed in their money, $125, and "pre-bid" for their chance at a new horse. It was first-come, first-selection. I signed up, knowing I would be number eighty-one—eighty people ahead of me would be able to chose their favorite horse. I was worried she'd be picked long before I had the chance to get her.

More bidders began trickling in, and by the end of the day over two-hundred people had deposited money, hoping to get a good mare, stallion or foal to take home and train.

I told the handlers I'd be keeping the horse at my neighbor's farm as he had a mustang enclosure from when he'd adopted his first two wild horses. I knew Rick would show up at the adoption, and when he did I begged him to let me keep her there until I could tame her and find a permanent barn.

"What makes you think you'll get her? You've got eighty people in front of you and she looks pretty good."

"If I don't, I won't take one. She's the only one I want."

It was true. Of all the horses in the pens, only the red horse with the pricked ears captured my heart. If I didn't get her I'd be crestfallen.

The following day bidders arrived at dawn, hoping to take home their favorites. Each of us had to write our desired horse's number on our bid sheet. If the horse was still available when our turn came, we got it. If it was already adopted, we could pick again.

My daughter dropped by to see the horse I had raved about the night before. As I led her to the pen, the curious little red horse with the pricked ears had changed. Her ears were to the side, her head lowered, and her coat had lost its luster.

"This is the one you want?" My daughter gave me that my-mother-has-lost-her-mind look.

"Well, she looked a lot better yesterday. I'm sure she's just tired." I was trying to convince myself, I think, as well as my daughter.

The first eighty bidders came and went, and not one of them wanted the little red mare with her head hung low. When the auctioneer called my number she was mine. It was almost too easy.

"Her name is Brandy," I beamed. He handed me my paperwork and pointed, sending me to the next table. There'd been no eye contact and no response to my beaming pronouncement.

After filling out a myriad of paperwork, it was time to take Brandy home. Wranglers forced her into a chute by waving white burlap bags at her. Once she was inside, men sitting on the rails deftly put a halter on her, snapped a lead line to it, and shooed her into Rick's horse trailer, where she joined the three horses Rick had purchased. We were on our way. I followed in my car, remembering one of the instructors saying, "Horses have been known to kick their way out of the trailers and run for miles." I kept watching for flying feet, but I could see the horses inside, standing quietly, as we drove along.

The trailer backed up to the barn and Rick opened the door. Four horses jumped out and into the barn, and Rick pulled a safety door down before they had a chance to turn around. As I walked inside and approached the stall containing the wild horses, two of them edged to the back and one tried climbing up the wall to get away from me. Brandy stood her ground. I extended my hand for her to sniff, and this time she did. Then she let me touch her soft nose.

I worked with her every day. The training went well—so well that we were able to saddle her and ride her after only a month. She never balked, never bucked, never made any attempt to hurt anyone. Soon I was able to move her to a different barn where the horses were turned out to a huge pasture every day and allowed to run from morning until night.

One evening I went over to help put the horses in. Rick whistled and called, but the horses did not want to give up their fun and come in, even though it meant supper. They were way back as far as the pasture could go, specks on the horizon, as happy as if they were in the wild, oblivious to the real world around them, and not thinking about humans, barns and stalls that protected them from the elements.

I climbed through the fence rails, put my hands on each side of my mouth to form a megaphone, and called …"BRANDY!" …. as loud as I could. Squinting, we saw heads go up. Then we heard the thunder of hoof beats.

"Well, I'll be damned," Rick said as Brandy appeared at the front of the pack. She ran like wildfire, jumping a small ditch like it was a puddle, and rushed over to the fence, shoving her face in mine. She pushed me with her head a couple of times, and I put my arms around her neck and gave her a big hug. I had been validated. Here, in front of all her equine friends and some humans as well, she came to my call. I knew we had a bond that could never be broken.

I finally bought my own farm, where she's the queen of the pasture. It's been fourteen years since that first push, and she's been giving me little nudges ever since, followed by a look that's the horse version of a wink. She has always delighted me with her eagerness to learn and her kindness to people and other animals. She has shared her stalls with ducklings and kittens, and she never harmed one of them.

I've always wondered if, on the day of the auction, she purposely put her ears to the side and lowered her head, knowing no one would bid on her in that pitiful condition. Could it be? I like to think so. And when I seem to take things for granted, Brandy gives me a little nudge to remind me of our special bond.

I AM YOUR DOG

Author Unknown

I am your dog, and I have a little something I'd like to whisper in your ear. I know that you humans lead busy lives. Some have to work, some have children to raise. It always seems like you are running here and there, often much too fast, often never noticing the truly grand things in life.

Look down at me now, while you sit there at your computer. See the way my dark brown eyes look at yours? They are slightly cloudy now. That comes with age. The gray hairs are beginning to ring my soft muzzle.

You smile at me; I see love in your eyes. What do you see in mine? Do you see a spirit? A soul inside, who loves you as no other could in the world? A spirit that would forgive all trespasses of prior wrong doing for just a simple moment of your time? That is all I ask. To slow down, if even for a few minutes to be with me. So many times you have been saddened by the words you read on that screen, of others of my kind, passing.

Sometimes we die young and oh so quickly; sometimes so suddenly it wrenches your heart out of your throat. Sometimes, we age so slowly before your eyes that you may not even seem to know until the very end, when we look at you with grizzled muzzles and cataract clouded eyes. Still the love is always there, even when we must take that long sleep, to run free in a distant land.

I may not be here tomorrow; I may not be here next week.

Someday you will shed the water from your eyes, the water that humans have when deep grief fills their souls, and you will be angry at yourself that you did not have just "One more day" with me. Because I love you so, your sorrow touches my spirit and grieves me. We have NOW, together. So come, sit down here next to me on the floor, and look deep into my eyes. What do you see? If you look hard and deep enough we will talk, you and I, heart to heart.

Come to me not as "alpha" or as "trainer" or even "Mom or Dad," come to me as a living soul and stroke my fur and let us look deep into one another's eyes, and talk. I may tell you something about the fun of chasing a tennis ball, or I may tell you something profound about myself, or even life in general.

You decided to have me in your life because you wanted a soul to share such things with. Someone very different from you, and here I am. I am a dog, but I am alive. I feel emotion, I feel physical senses, and I can revel in the differences of our spirits and souls. I do not think of you as a "Dog on two feet." I know what you are. You are human, in all your quirkiness, and I love you still.

Now, come sit with me, on the floor. Enter my world, and let time slow down if only for 15 minutes. Look deep into my eyes, and whisper to my ears. Speak with your heart, with your joy and I will know your true self. We may not have tomorrow, and life is oh so very short.

I'M STILL HERE

Author Unknown

Friend, please don't mourn for me
I'm still here, though you don't see.
I'm right by your side each night and day
and within your heart I long to stay.
My body is gone but I'm always near.
I'm everything you feel, see or hear.
My spirit is free, but I'll never depart
as long as you keep me alive in your heart.
I'll never wander out of your sight-
I'm the brightest star on a summer night.
I'll never be beyond your reach-
I'm the warm moist sand when you're at the beach.
I'm the colorful leaves when fall comes around
and the pure white snow that blankets the ground.
I'm the beautiful flowers of which you're so fond.
The clear cool water in a quiet pond.
I'm the first bright blossom you'll see in the spring,
The first warm raindrop that April will bring.
I'm the first ray of light when the sun starts to shine,
and you'll see that the face in the moon is mine.
When you start thinking there's no one to love you,
you can talk to me through the Lord above you.
I'll whisper my answer through the leaves on the trees,
and you'll feel my presence in the soft summer breeze.

I'm the hot salty tears that flow when you weep
and the beautiful dreams that come while you sleep.
I'm the smile you see on a baby's face.
Just look for me, friend, I'm everyplace!

ITTY BITTY – STORY OF A CHAMPION

By Avis Townsend

The day he was born I knew he was special. Son of a half-Arab, half pony mare and full Haflinger sire, the itty bitty little foal was full of pis-n-vinegar, ready to play at a moment's notice, vitality pouring out of him like a free-flowing fountain of youth. He was the same color as Brandy, my red mustang mare, right down to the white socks and the blaze down his nose. They were a matched set, one big the other small. When our eyes met, I knew I had to have him.

He belonged to the owners of the stable where I kept my horse. They'd be selling him as soon as he was weaned, or using him for their pony riding business. I hated the thoughts of him being worked for hire—he was way too happy. Inquiring about the cost if I bought him then and there, the owners gave me a quote. It was a little high, but I accepted it. This little guy was smart as a whip and was destined for greatness in the field of ponydom, I just knew it. And he didn't let me down.

Although his father was a miniature draft horse of sorts, and his mom half horse/half pony, the itty bitty guy was just plain tiny. The owners had named him Blaze, but how many million horses in the world sporting white stripes have been called Blaze?

He wasn't an ordinary Blaze. He was an itty bitty one. Thus, he was christened Itty Bitty by me. And though he's bypassed his mom's size and grown over the years, to me he will always be the Itty Bitty.

I recognized his intelligence when he was only three weeks old. The owners kept him and his mom in an area of their back yard. One side was bounded by the house, two other sides by fencing that surrounded the property. The fourth side, however, was two ropes, tied to the house on one side and the other fence on the other. About 100-feet long, the ropes sagged in the middle, the lower one on the ground more than off it, and the higher one remaining about three feet high. Itty learned that he could step over the low one and duck under the high one, and go off exploring on his own, much to the dismay of his mother, who spent most of her time gazing over the higher rope, helpless, calling her baby to come back to her.

After I'd decided to buy him, I introduced him to Brandy. She was about four at the time, and we don't think she'd ever had children, but being a wild horse, one never knows. She didn't have a pronounced "milk vein" seen by many broodmares after they'd delivered their offspring.

I walked brandy to the rope fence, making her stay on the opposite side of Itty's mom. Itty was immediately curious, and stepped carefully over the makeshift rope fence to have a look-see. Delighted that Brandy was a female, and a possible source of a well-needed drink, he immediately went to her side and dipped his face under, looking for that teat that would give him some warm milk. As he probed, Brandy's ears became flatter.

I was worried. Would she hurt him?

After another push with mouth and milk teeth, Itty Bitty found it confusing that this mother would have no milk. When he dove in for the final look, Brandy simply lifted a back leg and gave him a sidelong shove, about ten feet across the backyard, knocking him over to his side. He stood up, shook himself off, and trotted back under the fence to get that milk from his mom. From that day on, he respected Brandy as a stern aunt, and over the years they became best friends.

The day he was weaned was the first day he'd met a farrier. Not a good thing, mixing a day of heartbreak with a day of new things. We marched him into the barn, his squeals for his mom almost puncturing our ear drums, and the farrier grunted as he bent over, as low as he could go, to grab a foot. Itty Bitty wanted no part of that. Though four of us were holding him, he bucked, twisting and writhing, trying with all his might to get away. Finally, the barn owner lifted him off the ground, and with Itty's legs running in place, the farrier grabbed one at a time and did a little trim on each hoof. Once it was over and we let him down, he ran off, squealing and bucking in defiance, shaking his head at our rudeness, but he never objected to a farrier again. He'd shown his displeasure the first time around, but on the second attempt he figured he'd better grin and bear it, and the calmer he stood the faster it would go.

He was always one to learn things on the first try, and he was a joy to own. My favorite memories of his youth were watching him in an open field. His pasture antics were a pleasure to behold. He loved an audience, and if people walked down the road he gave them a great show. He'd trot along beside the fence, making sure they saw him. He'd do a few bucks, twist in place, squeal and run in circles, delighting his audience, quite pleased with himself and his performance.

However, if a person ignored him, he was more than offended, and he would snort and flare his nostrils, and run back and forth, bucking and kicking, parallel with the pedestrian's path, forcing them to look at him and acknowledge his presence.

My fondest pasture memory was when a Canada goose laid a nest of 16 eggs, right in the center of Itty's field. The first time he noticed them, he was standing about a hundred feet away. Suddenly his ears perked up and he arched his neck. What was that noise on the ground? He trotted over to the nest, sticking his nose on the eggs. The movement inside must have been clear to him, because he took off down the fence line, as fast as his legs would go, squealing and bucking, and when he circled to return to the nest, he pranced like his maternal grandfather and showed a bit of his Arabian heritage.

We moved Brandy and Itty to several stables before deciding to buy our own farm and be able to keep them at home. Although Brandy hated uprooting, each move was an adventure to Itty Bitty, and he loved searching every inch of new territory, looking for flowers to pick, bees to snort at, and soft grass to roll in.

We finally got our own place in 1995, when Itty was three – a fifty-acre farm in the middle of nowhere, with only two neighbors down the road. The neighbors had a boxer dog, and Itty and that dog played tag in the fields for months, while Brandy stood at a distance, too prim and proper to join in on the fun. I think she was relieved and grateful that Itty had someone else to bother, and allowed her to keep to herself, as prim and proper as she wanted to be.

Unfortunately, in the fall of that year Itty's boxer friend moved away, and Itty's playing days were over, except for a time or two each day when he'd run circles around Brandy, trying to get her to join in the fun. I don't know if it was his lack of exercise, or just nature taking a cruel turn, that caused him to contract laminitis, a painful attack of the feet. It's what killed the mighty Secretariat, and it downed my friend's mustang, Fire. But Itty Bitty was determined to fight it every inch of the way.

At first, the attacks came every few months. I'd know when he was suffering. He'd be slow in walking, lie down a lot, and breathe heavily when he touched each foot to the ground. I called the vet out with each emergency, but after a while I learned to deal with it myself.

No one knows what causes the disease, and though many have tried to find a cure, so far there is none. Not to go into great detail, the disease affects the lining of the hoof, the lamina, and it's said to make the horse feel like a woman would wearing a pair of high heels three sizes too small for a long period of time. Their feet feel pinched, and if let go and not treated, one of the bones in the foot can puncture the sole of the foot. The worse-case scenario is when the hoof wall crumbles away. When that happens, the horse must be euthanized immediately, as the pain is excruciating, and a horse can't stand without a foot.

I have been fighting the disease with him for nine years now. Many times, when it looked like the latest progression would not end and I would have to put him down, he'd bounce back, and the next few months would be spent frolicking once more in the pasture, playing with the four other stable mates I acquired since moving here.

Two years ago he suffered another bad attack, and spent almost two months lying down. Just when I thought it was time to call the vet to end the suffering, he bounced back, and he was good for over a year. Watching him running and playing, it scared me to think I could have ended his fun too early. Such a champion, he never let the pain get the better of him, and his will to live and run another day keeps forging onward.

As of this writing, we are going through another rough siege. It has been a horrible winter, one of the coldest on record. In Itty Bitty's case, cold weather brings on an attack. A few months ago I called the vet out, asking her if it was time to end things, and she said he seemed to be happy to be alive, and lying down a lot would make him comfortable.

"As long as he's eating and drinking, and seems to enjoy your company, he's not ready to be put down. Take it a day at a time," she advised.

During these past few months, there have been tears of sorrow, then tears of joy. He's taken me on a roller coaster ride of emotion—one day in the depths of pain, the next happy and silly. On the latest vet visit, I found out he has Cushing's disease, adding more fuel to the illness fire, but as long as he takes his medicine, he will be okay in that regard.

She also suggested I put some epoxy shoes on him. Two years ago, during his bad siege, John the farrier hammered corrective shoes on him, but the pain was so bad I could feel myself cringing, not wanting to do it anymore. It was heartbreaking watching him suffer the horrendous blows of the hammer.

"Don't do that again," the vet advised. "It's way too painful. If he needs shoes again, we'll temporarily block the nerves in his feet so he can't feel the nails. But try epoxy ones first. They glue on, and there's no pain."

I asked the farrier to order the shoes.

Fortunately, it was good timing. John was going to a farrier's convention, getting apprised of the latest in technology. He didn't let me down. After the convention, he stopped by with a suitcase filled with polyvinyl shoes, and the adhesive to stick them to the foot. All was well with the world. Or was it? After trying for two hours, there was no way the shoes would stick.

There is more involved with these shoes than just gluing them on. First they must be soaked in very hot water to make them pliable. Hooves must be trimmed, to the extent of filing down the hoof wall in front so shoes could adhere better.

It took an hour to trim and file his feet. Then, it took several minutes to soak the shoe, which is a white polyvinyl plastic. John squirted the glue inside the shoe via a special applicator that came with the kit. Then he had to hold the foot up in the air for five minutes. This was difficult. At one point, Itty came off the ground with both back feet while John held the foot being shod. Finally, when the foot went down to the floor of the barn, the shoe came off. The glue was not sticking. John tried four times. He was swearing profusely by the end of the trial, Itty Bitty was getting tired, I was getting frantic.

"We're going to Plan B," John said, walking outside to his truck and coming back with flat metal shoes and regular epoxy glue. They wouldn't stick either. After more than two hours, nothing was accomplished except all of us being tired and upset.

The salesmen, who came to the United States from England just to display the shoes, would be at the convention the next day, John said. He was going to find them and bring them to the barn.

The next day, however, John returned alone. The English guys stiffed him at the farrier's convention, and when he called their hotel, the hotel manager said they weren't taking calls. This left him worried after buying the special shoes. But, VISA called him and asked if it was okay to let the charge for the shoes go through, seeing as how he charged in the United States one minute and the next minute the charge went through the UK. He didn't call back VISA immediately, waiting to see if the shoes would work or if he got taken. If it was the latter, he wouldn't approve the transaction.

So, on the second day he tried again, using the British epoxy in the foot of the shoe, and his own epoxy for the area around the hoof. For some reason, everything worked. Whether it was because it was warmer in the barn than the day before, all of us weren't as tired, or a miracle happened, I don't know. But it worked.

The new shoes are uglier than heck, but who cares? For white plastic shoes, the cement provided by the company was also white, and the photo in the brochure shows a horse wearing two lovely new shoes. In our case, John used he white glue for inside the shoe, and smeared black regular epoxy on the outside. Hideous, but it worked. At this stage of the game we aren't worrying about appearances.

I went out to the barn the next morning and all shoes were still on his feet, and he was standing up, waiting for breakfast. Usually he is lying down, waiting until the last minute until he gets up to eat.

As of this writing, my wonderful Itty Bitty is still alive. The day after the shoes went on, I looked out the window and saw him playing with Jack, our donkey. He hadn't played in months. As he's only twelve years old, and because he loves life more than any animal or human I know, I will do anything I can to keep him happy and alive.

My vet said I'll know when he's no longer happy, and I have the spot picked out where he will be buried. I don't want him to die, but I don't want his quality of life to decline to the point that he is sad and miserable, and constantly in pain. He's too much of a champion for that, just like the mighty Secretariat.

An autopsy showed that Secretariat had a huge heart, one that kept him forging onward, being the fastest horse in history. I'm sure Itty Bitty has an equally large heart, enabling him to forget the pain, push onward, looking for new adventures and friends to play with.

I'm so glad I decided to take him all those years ago. If his former owners had kept him, they'd have sent him to "the meater" at the first time his feet flared up. "Can't have a horse with bad feet," they'd say over and over, loading their poor sick horses on a trailer, heading off to stock yards to be killed for dog food or human consumption in France. I am eternally grateful each day that I had the chance to keep him going, even though the cost was great, and share in the spirit he so eagerly lavishes on all who visit him.

My friend says when the time comes I'll be able to stand with him in his final moments, waiting for the veterinarian's shot to take his pain away for evermore. I don't know about that. I'm skeptical. I begin crying just thinking about having to make that decision. To stand with this friend I've had for all his life – a friend who's amazed and delighted me with his antics – and help him cross over to greener pastures, I don't know if I'm that strong. I guess time will tell.

Perhaps these shoes are the magical cure. Perhaps he'll live another twenty or so years, frolicking in the pasture, munching away at hay and treats, and he'll die peacefully in his sleep some warm summer evening. It's a dream to hang onto.

JOSH – DEFENDER OF YOUTH

By Amy L. Jenkins

Funny thing about naming your dog Josh. You can't yell at him. If you try, the s-h sounds coming from your own voice, JO..SH, tells you to knock it off. Anyway, why would anyone yell at Josh?

My mom got him out of a cardboard box at the gas station when I was about 13. The owner was giving him away. He was mostly collie, and we thought some shepherd too. It was the early 70's, and we never thought of having him fixed. Sometimes his testosterone got the best of him and he'd go visiting all over the neighborhood. Once he was gone for a half-hour and a guy brought him back after reading his dog tag.

"How long was he missing?" our stranger asked, "He sure was hungry, we gave him the rest of our roast, and a plate of biscuits—boy did he wolf it down." I just hugged our renegade, who happily pelted me with his tail, and left my Dad to mumble a thankful response.

I loved Josh, and he loved me. I believed he loved me the most, because he slept in my room. When he lay on the floor next to my bed, he took up the whole floor. If someone opened the door, they'd bang into him. One Saturday morning, a designated clean-up-the-house day, I heard my Mom coming towards my room. I turned to face the wall to facilitate the "I'm still sleeping" act. As the door opened, Josh began a primal growl. He kept growling and I knew he was showing his teeth, maybe his eyes were even glowing red. My mom closed the door. I smiled at the wall I strained to hear her mutter, with the volume descending as she walked down the hall, "I guess Josh thinks it's too early to get up."

In our family, the kids didn't have too many rights. Kids were second class citizens. If we'd had a bus, kids would have been required to sit in the back.

When company came to watch the game, we didn't set up extra chairs; the kids sat on the floor. At Thanksgiving, the kids' dinner was eaten at a card table. We spoke when we were spoken to, and we were a bit afraid of our parents. If you were the little sister, your big sister always got the bigger half of the candy bar, the bigger room, and Mom liked her better.

I had gone through my grade school years with the civil rights movement all around me, so as my hormones kicked in, it was easy to naively translate the oppression I had heard about to my situation. The youngest kids are always the most oppressed members of a family and some day we would rise up, I imagined, and claim our American birth right of equality.

But Josh slept by my bed, not my sister's, and he growled at Mom, never at me. When you're thirteen and know more than anyone, and you're sure that most things are stupid, unfair and boring, it's great to have a dog who loves you. Because when you're thirteen, sometimes nobody else can.

Author's Bio: Amy Jenkins is a nurse and writer from Milwaukee, Wisconsin. She writes creative nonfiction and heath care articles. She's been widely published in regional and national magazines, and anthologized in four books. She loves anthologies and serves as editor for *www.AnthologiesOnline.com*. She is studying for her MFA in Creative Writing at Bennington College.

MAJA, A STRIPED TABBY

By Roberta Beach Jacobson, Karpathos Greece

Maja, a striped tabby, was born in the Darmstadt, Germany Tierheim (animal shelter) on a late September day. The placement with her first adoptive family was not a successful one, so back to the animal shelter she went. Things went along fine with her second family - until the human baby came along, that is. Once again, Maja was whisked back to the animal shelter. The adoption contract specifies any pet must be returned if the match is not a good one.

By her third adoption, Maja was pretty used to being shuffled around. She was going on six years old by then. As it turned out, somebody in that family had an allergy to cats, so Maja's stay in the household was a short-lived one. I first met little Maja on a cold December day when I made my first solo visit to the busy shelter to see the cats. Several seemed to accept me a little, but most pretended indifference to my visit. It did not go smoothly with all the cats I met. One 14-year-old toothless black cat, recently orphaned when his elderly human mother passed away, tried to gum me out of his private room. He wanted to snooze in the sun - alone. It was clear he wanted me to leave.

Maja lived in a room with about eight other adult cats. She appeared cool, curiously observing me from a safe distance. The one time she allowed me to pet her, she purred. A shelter worker looked through her file and informed me Maja was to be placed only with a family without other cats, and certainly one without any dogs or human children. She was to be an only child. Period!

I rushed home and briefed my husband on the few cats who seemed to at least be able to tolerate me. I handed him a list with the names of three kitties.

Our plan was that he would go to the shelter alone later that same afternoon, meet all the cats and then make a choice.

He came home with Maja! We had all the basic kitty necessities ready - litter box and sand, scratching post, bed, food and water dishes. The shelter's contract was four pages long, basically holding Alf (my husband) accountable for all aspects of Maja's overall well being. It recorded the tattooed number in her ears - to be used for identification purposes as well as to guarantee her future safety. (It is forbidden in Germany for any labs to buy any such tattooed dogs or cats.)

The contract also specified that Maja was to be examined by a vet at least annually. Any social adjustment problems had to be brought to the attention of the shelter immediately and Alf could not give or sell Maja to any third party if her adoption wasn't working out. In that case, Maja was to be returned to the shelter. The contact also contained a clause stating that they expected periodic written development reports (photos encouraged) on our newest family member. The detailed contract wasn't the only paperwork we received, but also Maja's medical and shot records. She had been spayed at the age of eight months, also a strict requirement for all shelter animals in Germany.

About a month after Maja joined us, a shelter volunteer came for an unannounced home visit. She surveyed Maja's eating area, her bed, toys and kitty box. She examined the uncooperative tabby, poking around for any signs of physical abuse - much to Maja's extreme dislike. Maja did not warm up to this intruder from the shelter and soon retreated to the comfort of her basket where nobody would bother her.

The volunteer quizzed me at length about our cat's eating and sleeping habits and reviewed Maja's shelter contract and medical file. I was reminded that Maja was due for shots the following month and that I should also submit a stool sample to the vet at the same time.

A couple weeks after I'd phoned one of our town's two vets to get Maja scheduled for a complete physical and shots, an animal shelter representative called us to make sure we'd tended to her medical needs. I gave her our appointment date, assuring her I was watching out for the cat's health needs.

It was quite an ordeal to adopt Maja. She has now been with us for eight years and we all know we did the right thing.

Author's Bio: Roberta Beach Jacobson is an American writer who has lived in Europe for the past 30 years. She comes from Lake in the Hills, Illinois, but now makes her home on the remote Greek island of Karpathos. Her pet articles have appeared in *I Love Cats*, *PoodlePress.com*, *Just Cats!*, *ILoveDogs.net* and *Cats Magazine*. Her website is http://www.travelwriters.com/Roberta.

MOONPIE, A GIANT PERSIAN

By Marilyn Ure

One of my favorite cats was a giant Persian I named Moonpie.

I found him loitering outside my kitchen window. He scared the be-jeebies out of me, looking like a giant Weok – a great big fluffy cat with a smashed-in face.

He wouldn't let me get near him. He found his way into our garage, where he hid from all humans. I started taking little bits of turkey to him, to try to lure him out. This did the trick. He came out for the turkey, each day a little farther, until finally he let me pick him up. It was obvious to be he'd been mistreated, and he had no trust for humans. He didn't trust me, anyway – that was obvious. His paw could fly out with lightning speed and nail anyone with those giant claws of his.

He was a mess…his fur was matted and tearing off his body in large clumps.

I knew I had to get him to the vets and get that hair shaved off, to give him some relief.

After about a week, he trusted me enough that I could take him to the groomer's. By this time, he developed an infection on his skin where the hair had fallen off. He tore up the groomer pretty good, and we decided he'd need to be sedated before she could touch him again.

I made Moonpie my mission in life…to get him to trust me enough to at least pet him. It took several months of patience, but he finally got to the point where he would come up to my room and lay on me to sleep. But, every once in a while that paw would come out and get me, just to remind me who was boss.

He died under my bed one day, and it was a very sad day for me. I can still imagine him walking up the stairs on his final journey before passing to the other side. And I still miss him.

His ashes are buried under a beautiful rose bush, and each spring when the roses come in bloom, I know they are blooming with love over my wonderful Moonpie.

Author's bio: Marilyn Ure lives in Henderson, Nevada, with her husband and one son who still remains at home. She has six children, three grandchildren, six cats ("at the moment") and one very spoiled Cocker spaniel. Her interests include tarot card reading, dancing, gardening, riding her Harley, teaching piano and, of course, taking care of her animals.

PAULY-WAULY-DOODLE

By Nina M. Osier

"I've lost my home. Will you take me in?"

The big yellow-and-white tomcat had seen better days. His dignified manner demonstrated that. So did his understanding of what being housebroken meant, when Jimmy Osier tried letting the skinny but muscular feline inside. After all, the solitary clam digger reasoned, his unfinished four-room cottage could survive an accident or two if this animal didn't yet know the etiquette required of a house pet. But "Paul," as Jimmy christened him, never once sprayed the furniture or made a mess on the linoleum floor.

By asking his few neighbors, Jimmy soon learned that Paul had been allowed inside until just a few months earlier. But when the cat's owner (an elderly lobsterman from the Maine island's other side) passed away, family members settling the old man's estate didn't trouble themselves about anything as unimportant as a now homeless and bewildered animal.

So Paul the feline made his way across the island's frozen snowdrifts, from the house where no one let him in or fed him anymore, until he came at last to Jimmy Osier's little cottage. The troubled war veteran lived there, cut off from the mainland and civilization by half a mile of salt water, whenever he needed to get away from everything - his young family included. In that cottage (or "camp," as he was far more likely to call it), he and Paul were soon living the bachelor's life together.

Clearly the big tom had had some difficult experiences during his months as a refugee. At first Jimmy didn't dare to touch him, because Paul feared human hands and struck out whenever they came too near. The cat meant business, too. Yet he was well behaved in every other way, making pleasant company for a man who'd always been fond of felines. Had Friendship Long Island's other residents violently

107

rebuffed Paul's attempts to take shelter in their homes, or just to find scraps on their trash heaps? It looked that way to Jimmy. One evening when Paul leaped onto his chest, as he lay on the sofa and read a book by the light from a kerosene lamp, he didn't dare to move. If he put up a hand to remove the cat, he risked being slashed.

Or so he thought - but by then Paul had learned to trust his new human. Several hours after the cat landed and settled down to nap, Jimmy cautiously reached up to stroke him. Instead of ripping the hand that was touching his fur, Paul started purring. Loudly and contentedly.

Paul had a fine life after that. Whenever Jimmy sold clams or sea moss (his two main sources of cash), he and Paul shared a steak dinner; and he made sure that his cat ate regularly, although not as grandly, the rest of the time. Paul played the role of companion and confidant, listening with patient interest to his human's comments and troubles. Since Jimmy loved to make puns, he often addressed the feline musically as: "Pauly-Wauly-Doodle! All the day!"

When summer came, and Jimmy's wife joined them for part of her school teaching vacation, he wondered how Paul would accept her because the cat continued to be suspicious of most visitors. But Paul took to Marie immediately, as if he'd never had a reason to expect cruelty from the female half of humanity.

What to do with Paul, when fall arrived and Jimmy decided it was finally time to go home? No one on the island wanted another cat, and he didn't even think about taking the unaltered tom to live in the city with his family. Surely Paul would get by on his own. He had before, after all. Cats always did, didn't they?

When he came back to the island the following summer, Jimmy asked for news about Paul. "The yellow tomcat you took in?" his across-the-cove neighbor responded. "Oh, sure, I know where he is. He's dead."

"What happened?" Jimmy wanted to know, by then wishing that he'd done something - anything - except abandon the animal. Just like Paul's previous owner, from the unfortunate cat's viewpoint.

"I saw him and a bunch of other toms going after each other over a fish skin, sometime back in the winter," the neighbor said. "Must of been pretty hungry, to fight like that for a scrap. He wouldn't let it go, and a stronger tom wound up killing him."

So the magnificent cat who'd grown sleek and powerful on the good food Jimmy fed him, who slept on his human's bed and answered with an affectionate "Meow!" to whimsical choruses of "Pauly-Wauly-Doodle!", died fighting for possession of a fish skin. Starving, and too weak to win his final battle.

That's why Jimmy Osier never again believed what he'd been taught in boyhood, that a cat can always get its living from somewhere. It's also why he taught his own children that if you can no longer take care of a pet yourself, you must make other arrangements. No matter how inconvenient that may be!

Author bio: Nina ("9-UH") M. Osier started writing at the age of two, when her parents transcribed her stories and read them back to her. She lives in Augusta, Maine, where she directs the Maine State Archives Division of Records Management Services, obeys the wishes of her six cats, gardens, and never gets enough sleep. Her latest book, "Love, Jimmy: A Maine Veteran's Longest Battle," was released by Writers Club Press in January, 2003.

PEANUT

By: Sandy Williams Driver

The veterinarian looked at me with disgust in his eyes that Monday morning as he made his diagnosis: Parvo.

I suddenly became defenseless and felt the need to explain to him that contrary to what it may seem, I was a responsible pet owner. I knew the Parvo virus was an intestinal disease which attacked dogs, mainly puppies, who hadn't been properly vaccinated. But, had Peanut been given his shots? I really didn't know.

The previous Thursday, I had picked up a copy of the local newspaper and scanned the classified ads in search of a small puppy to occupy the large fenced backyard of our new home. My heart skipped a beat when I read: "Free, male dachshund/basset hound mix puppy, only eight weeks old." I hurriedly dialed the number fearing someone else had already beaten me and whisked the little fellow away.

I was ecstatic when the kindly old man told me no one else had called as of yet and gave me directions to his home. When I drove up and saw an adorable black and tan puppy struggling to walk down the front steps, I knew I had found something to fill the void in my children's lives.

I asked about any vaccinations already given, but the man became vague and told me he couldn't remember if his wife had taken the litter of pups for their first round of shots or not. She wasn't at home to question, but it made no matter to me. A free puppy this cute was a rare find so I made plans to take him to the veterinarian first thing Monday morning.

Our whole family stayed up late that night playing with Peanut and showing him around his new home. After dropping my three children off at school the next morning, I returned to find our new puppy lying on the porch, sound asleep.

Assuming he was tired from the previous night's activities, I decided to let him rest while I attended to a few of my daily chores.

That afternoon, the children were disappointed to find Peanut still lying down and not wanting to play with them. I explained he was probably depressed from being separated from his mother and siblings. I was a little concerned when he ate only a few bites of puppy food and drank just a sip of water and my anxiety grew when he continued the same behavior the following day.

On Sunday, I anticipated him to be in better spirits, but he took a sudden turn for the worse around mid-afternoon when he began vomiting and having diarrhea. He refused to eat and even rejected the water we gave him to drink. He became critically ill within a few short hours.

Throughout the afternoon and night, my husband and I took turns sitting with Peanut and kept him as dry and warm as possible. We were very sad and worried about this little guy whom we had only known for three days but had already found a place in our hearts.

On Monday, the veterinarian diagnosed him with Parvo and informed us that apparently our puppy had never been given any vaccinations. The outlook for survival was dim as he hooked up an IV to try and replenish some of the fluids lost from vomiting and diarrhea and maintain hydration. We went home to prepare our children for what we thought at the time was inevitable.

Peanut stayed in the animal hospital for three days. We visited him each afternoon to cheer him up and show him we hadn't forgotten about him. We were surprised by how much weight he had lost so quickly and how lifeless he appeared by Wednesday afternoon.

When the veterinarian informed us his office would be closed over the next four days for the Thanksgiving holidays, we became troubled. He assured us someone from the staff would make regular visits twice a day to check on the animals and administer their medications, but we decided it wasn't enough.

Armed with a bag of medications and a list of instructions, we wrapped Peanut up in a blanket and took him home. We spent Thanksgiving Day forcing small white antibiotic pills and liquid doses of anti-vomiting medicine down our little pup's throat. We gave him syringes full of Pediatric Pedialyte to regulate his electrolyte levels and coaxed sips of water down his throat to prevent dehydration.

We kept clean newspapers in the bottom of the big box he slept in and gave him a fresh towel to cuddle against whenever he soiled the previous one. A night-light and a radio were both kept on in the den whenever we left the room to reassure him he wasn't alone. Our whole family took turns holding him, talking to him and loving him.

We were awakened on Saturday morning by a welcoming sound: a high-pitched barking. It was a noise we hadn't heard for six days and we all rushed down to the den. We were overjoyed to see Peanut standing up against the side of the box and wagging his tail. He was one of the lucky survivors of the dreadful disease and he slowly began his recovery. As instructed by the veterinarian, we fed him a bland diet over the next week before gradually resuming his normal diet. Peanut is now a mature, healthy and happy dog who survived a fatal disease thanks to the medication supplied by our veterinarian and our family's loving care.

Author's bio: Sandy Williams Driver, and her husband, Tim, live in Albertville, Alabama, where both were born and raised. They have three children: Josh, Jake and Katie. Sandy is a full-time homemaker and a part-time writer. Her short stories and essays have appeared in numerous magazines all over the world and have been included in several anthologies. She also writes a weekly parenting column for her local newspaper, *The Sand Mountain Reporter*.

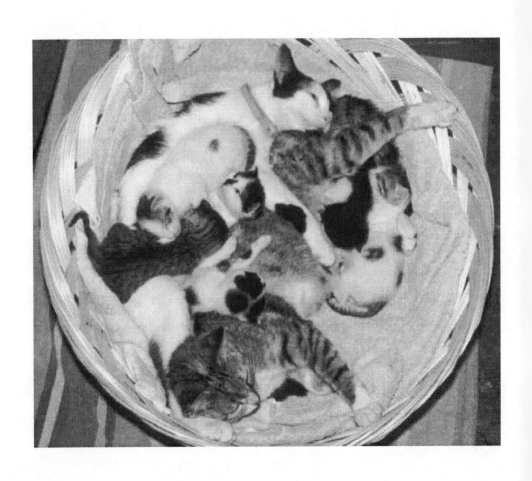

PET LIFE IN GREECE

And the feral cats that adopt the humans

By Roberta Beach Jacobson

Athens has a sad stray problem and needs to do something about 20,000 - 30,000 street dogs that have a really horrible life.

The current plan (part of the let's get ready for the Olympics visitors, who can't be tripping over dogs sleeping all over the sidewalks) is to catch, neuter and label (put a chip in) each dog. The first plan was the horrendous announcement they would simply shoot them all and the public, of course, rebelled.

So the spaying and chipping is the latest plan and it's underway. The thing is, days later the dogs then get released back to the streets, same as before. True, the population will go down eventually. This is very, very important, but this plan doesn't feed or care for the dogs once they're back on the city streets!

People there had until June, 2004, to get their pets to the vets to pay for a chip, and all other dogs are to be considered strays. I wish some of these stray dogs could find safe and loving families, that people would put their money where their mouths are, so to speak. What's lacking is people who want the responsibility of pets, coupled with the absence of shelters to help out. There are vets in Greece, but primarily located in cities. Shelters are virtually unknown.

Most of us who live on remote islands, which is much of the population of this country, generally have few doctors of any type. On our little island of Karpathos, we have four dentists, but no vets!! We don't understand how our dogs will get their chips, and there is a big fine if a pet dog is not chipped by a certain date.

Cats are not to be chipped in the government's new program.

We live in a farming village (population 150) way up in the hills, with only walking paths connecting the houses. There is no road nearby. The sole street runs to each town, but this isn't generally the spot where people live. So our neighborhood is an ideal location for cats and dogs. Since I experienced a special kitten getting run over (decades ago, but I will never forget it), I am very happy in the safety factor of being car-free. In fact, one reason we liked this old farmhouse or this area in general was the assumed safety for pets. They have lots of space to romp around, plenty of trees to climb, mice to catch, and lots to explore while outside.

Dogs here are not put on leashes – they run free. And there are goats, sheep, chickens and a donkey right near out house. So, it's sort of a loud zoo atmosphere – just with no car noises added to it.

We brought our old, essentially indoor cat with us in our move here in 1999 and she adapted to the outside quickly. We couldn't believe the transformation. All the strays wanted the chance to sleep inside and our cat suddenly wanted to sleep outside and explore. She never saw so many bugs and fun stuff. And she caught her first mouse at age 11 or 12. Here we'd worried this place might be too "wild" for her!

We estimate most cats here live three years on average. But that's due to receiving no meds (not even the basic shots) and many felines get colds in the damp winters. And they get in horrible fights or get injured (scorpions, etc.).

We moved here in September and the first winter we removed all tools from the shed (used to be an outhouse in days of old) and built ugly shelves out of old wood and placed ripped blankets, unwanted toilet lid covers in all colors, old towels, etc. in there. We used some old dresser drawers along the bottom row. Not at all attractive to look at, but okay for keeping off the rain. I flea-powdered the sleeping areas, as the cats were infested with fleas. I tried some direct treatment and almost lost my arm. Worms I can't do much for with the wild cats. I wouldn't get near their mouths with either the pills or the squirty stuff.

The shed worked okay when our numbers were relatively small, but then so many cats had litters. They start early (eight months isn't unusual) and have three litters a year. Of course, a high percentage of kittens do not make it. Their mothers are too young, weak, tired from always having babies, not well fed - just not up to it. But as time went on and we fed and fed (and fed) and gave our indoor cats medicines, well, more kittens survived. And more cats came inside to have their litters and then they became house cats and never left. And their babies never left either. We have three generations of some cat families.

Once we had 17 cats in the house, and before long it was 24 and then 31. I remember the numbers because we used flea collars back then, not anti-flea/tick drops on the neck. For safety reasons (getting stuck in trees), we stopped flea collars and now keep enormous lists of who gets what medicine.

The next step after the shed was that cats could sleep in the bathroom or office (going outside and in through open windows), and that worked fine for small groups for rainy overnights. But it was not a long-term solution Having a cat flap added to our problem, as a year or two later the cat population just seemed to expand everywhere under our feet. They took over our house, room by room. We aren't fast or smart enough to keep the wild ones out, so now we have to have litter boxes for the younger ones - just in case. We thought we'd never have one of those things again! As it is now, a whole bunch of our band sleeps in the bed. My husband tells me we should go live in the shed and simply give the cats our house.

Luck was on our side, I guess. Some German vets came here on vacation, saw all the strays and returned to do something about the situation. The main volunteer vet, Martina, has adopted eleven cats from the island, all the three-legged and blind and ones with quite major problems. Now she has pharmaceutical firms as sponsors who donate medications for the cause. The program has developed to the point where vets can come twice a year. They handle not only neutering, but emergency surgery, routine immunizations and general pet care. I can't thank Martina and her helpers enough. Without her caring and selfless attitude (she sometimes even pays for her own flight), we'd be in the dog house - literally. Other firms have donated sacks of food, but we're having a hard time arranging transport.

In between vet visits we always had new kittens. This was before we got donated supplies of birth control pills and shots. I was worried we were going to end up with a hundred cats, I really was. It scared me to think it was so out of control and we'd keep having to feed more and more. I told my husband we were not truly helping them (or ourselves) by simply feeding and being kind to them. They needed to be fixed, fixed, fixed. The cycle had to end. More and more cats were showing up at our door and the poor mother cats were nursing and half the neighborhood toms were after them already.

So, four months after giving birth, they'd be having yet another litter. Martina has done a lot for us. One spring alone we had 17 of "our" cats neutered.

There are many people here who would love to set up a formal shelter for the island's unwanted cat and dog population. But we can't to this without having a building and professional medical care. It just doesn't matter how much good we intend to do or how many volunteers we find. We would definitely need doctors.

Our cats are almost famous. In summer, tourists walk right in our courtyard to take pictures of our dozens of snoozing kitties. It's really funny. Once I found a

Dutch woman climbing our almond tree because she said a cat was stuck. I think the cat was just sitting there. But she went up and got it down.

I have a couple of problem cases within the feral colony: When the vets have been here, I've been pretty successful at catching them and bribing the cats into cages. After they are neutered, they need to recuperate. Otherwise they'd wobble down the steps or over a cliff. So we allow these cats sleep inside for 16 or 18 hours or however long they need. And most (I'd say 90%) never leave. They adopt us. Most of our older cats have come to us in this exact way. Then, weeks after they got neutered, they tamed down. They observe the other household feline behavior and many adapt.

We've had some huge cats I truthfully was afraid of before and now they happily snooze on my desk or in our living room chairs. One white male had bitten us both (drawing a lot of blood) quite seriously. I thought he was a horrible creature. Once castrated, some of these jumbo feral cats can turn into easy pets, never asking for anything special. They eat and they sleep indoors and they learn to relax and play. Some even trust us enough to sit on our laps – low-maintenance cats, we call them. You could never predict such an outcome from seeing them in their original outside environment, ears all chewed up, scratched all over - mean and hissing things.

I guess it proves that a little love goes a long way.

(Author's bio is attached to the other story, Maja, a Striped Tabby)

PETS AND AGING – SOME ANIMAL ADVICE

By Kimberly J. Stauder, Webster Groves, Missouri

It is a weekend morning like hundreds of other weekend mornings. I roll over and awaken my two companions, Heidi, the small, longhaired dachshund, and Boots, the huge black and white cat. Once awake, we begin a rousing game of "Hand". Both animals attempt to chase and bite my fingers under the blanket. There is a great deal of growling, and whining, as the three of us jockey for position on the bed. Heidi and I eventually take our tussle to the floor. We try to outwit each other as we roll and dive across the carpet. Our shrieks of laughter and barking make the struggles sound much more intense than they actually are.

The years are catching up with us. I am fifty years old, Heidi is sixteen, and Boots is the baby at fourteen. Although my pets tire more quickly of the games than in years past, they still continue to approach them with great enthusiasm. It is our special time when my companions don't have to share me with the world of responsibilities outside my bedroom. Our early morning fun is reminiscent of my childhood years when my brother and I would roughhouse on our beds long before our parents awoke.

As I stare into Heidi's little white face, the only sign of her advancing years, I am suddenly aware that my little dog doesn't know she is old. Time has stood still for her as it has for the cat. Neither Heidi nor Boots have any idea how many playtime mornings have gone by or how many lay ahead. It is very apparent to me how much my pets can teach me about aging gracefully.

Lessons on Aging as Lived By Heidi and Boots

Sleep when you are tired…my pets never have two or three more things to do before they can take a nap or hit the sack for the night.

Stretch and stay limber…Boots and Heidi always awake from sleeping with long, luxurious stretches.

Exercise regularly…Heidi and I still take long walks around the neighborhood, although the word *brisk* is no longer part of our vocabulary. The cat stays home where his daily exercise consists of numerous trips from the basement to the second floor and back.

Get proper medical care and always take your medication…the calendar is noted with pet wellness visits. We make frequent trips to the special cat clinic and to the dog's favorite vet. The kitchen shelf is lined with various medications. There are pills for Heidi's stiff joints, heartworm prevention, and flea guard. Boots takes a red pill for his kidneys and a little white pill to keep him mellow, and ensure that he will use his litter box. One morning about six months ago, I accidentally swallowed his white pill. I was pleasantly laid back as I realized I wouldn't relieve myself on the carpet that day!

Watch your diet and savor the treats …Boots is on a special kidney food minus all protein. He gets one small piece of cheese a day with his pills buried inside. He eats it very slowly while constantly licking his lips and purring. Heidi is also on a special diet. The early years meant yummy puppy chow, followed by a less tasty maintenance food, followed by a dry light food and finally a dusty senior version. The pill she takes for her joints is a chewable, and judging from her reaction the highlight of her daily dining experience.

Don't let your infirmities stand in your way. Live your life as normally as you can…Boots drinks enormous amounts of water due to his kidney problem. I simply added a litter box to all levels of the house so the big guy can still enjoy all his special sleeping spots. A few years ago, the dog lost most of her hearing. For sixteen years, she has been stubborn and independent. Now Heidi is treating her infirmity as a late life blessing and using it to the fullest advantage. She frequently runs off exploring the backyard and the flowerbeds knowing that I won't even bother to reprimand her. After all, I feel rather silly standing on the deck, scolding a dog that the neighbors know is stone deaf.

Make sure you stay warm in cold weather…after Heidi understood the value of her green sweater she began bringing it to me before every trip outside in the winter chill. Boots has managed to find the three or four warmest areas of our home and regularly rotates between them.

Make the best of the heat and humidity…absolutely no amount of coaxing will get the cat to go outdoors when the temperatures are soaring. Boots realizes the benefits of limiting your exercise and staying put. If left unattended in the yard, invariably the dog will find the coolest spot, a mud puddle left over from the morning sprinklers.

Go out and play in the snow whenever you have the chance… but get someone else to shovel it…whenever we have a snowfall of three inches or more the household is in trouble because Heidi only has three-inch legs. Charlie, the young man across the street, shovels an area of the backyard about six feet square for my little dog as she stands on the deck supervising the entire job while barking profusely.

Learn to appreciate the freedom a good chauffer provides…both pets love to jump in the car (yes, a cat in the car) and go places knowing that they are safe and secure. They use the time in the car to play, look out the windows as the world zips by, or to just take a quick little snooze. Car rides are fun and relaxing without any responsibilities.

Make friends with your fears…after a decade of running in terror from the vacuum cleaner, both pets have finally made peace with the wicked machine. Now they barely raise their heads when I vacuum.

Stand your ground when you feel your opinion matters…Everyday for sixteen years I have been pinning Heidi to the floor to brush her teeth. I am completely exhausted when we are through and never quite sure if the toothbrush reached all of her teeth. Boots has remained as opinionated as the dog. He hates the vet no matter who the vet is. He used to only moan, however, in later years he has added wild, continuous shrieking that scatters everyone in his path. It starts when we open the door to go inside the clinic and quits the minute we leave.

Stay close to those that are important to you...Both pets love to follow me
around. They remain firmly planted at my feet as if I'm going to get lost.
Tripping has become a new pastime for me.

Finally, lose all concept of time and live for today...my dog and cat don't
know one day or one year from the next. They don't worry about the past or
the future. Their entire world consists of what is happening right now. This is
why every weekend morning still finds them full of joy and enthusiasm zestfully
starting the day with a good game of "Hand".

Author's Bio: Kimberly Stauder writes a monthly pet column for a local periodical
in addition to contributing articles to *Petwarmers.com* and other on-line magazines.
She resides in historic Webster Groves, MO with her constant, Four-Legged
traveling companion, Dagny, a small wired-haired dachshund, who has heard
endless stories of Heidi and Boots. Kimberly is co-owner of Nuwati Herbals,
Inc., an all-natural herbal company that creates and manufactures products for
humans and their Four-Legged friends.

RESCUE ME

Author Unknown

Rescue me not only with your hands but with your heart as well.
I will respond to you.
Rescue me not out of pity but out of love.
I will love you back.
Rescue me not with self-righteousness but with compassion.
I will learn what you teach.
Rescue me not because of my past but because of my future.
I will relax and enjoy.
Rescue me not simply to save me but to give me a new life.
I will appreciate your gift.
Rescue me not only with a firm hand but with tolerance and patience.
I will please you.
Rescue me not only because of who I am but who I'm to become.
I will grow and mature.
Rescue me not to revere yourself to others but because you want me.
I will never let you down.
Rescue me not with a hidden agenda but with a desire to teach me to
trust.
I will be loyal and true.
Rescue me not to be chained or to fight but to be your companion.
I will stand by your side.
Rescue me not to replace one you've lost but to soothe your spirit.

I will cherish you.
Rescue me not to be your pet but to be your friend.
I will give you unconditional love.
Please Rescue Me!

SHANNA, A STORY OF LOVE, DEVOTION AND COURAGE

By Dana Smith-Mansell

Every one of my pets is special to me. Each has brought pleasure and enlightenment into my life. I have learned something from each one of them, and have received an abundance of love. I can only hope that on some level, I have given them a piece of what they have given to me. All have left me with a gift, a lesson, a memory. I am blessed to have had each one in my life, as I know they were a gift from God. Shanna was my first gift, and the last months of her life filled me with tremendous anguish, and personal and spiritual growth. I never expected to learn life's most intensive lessons from a dog, but I did.

Shanna was a West Highland White Terrier and was full of spunk and tenacity from the moment I saw her. As I looked at her through the window at the pet shop, she stared right into my eyes, and at the moment I felt an uncanny connection. She did not break eye contact and her tail wagged furiously. She followed me as I strolled past the other dogs, almost stretching her neck to keep me in view. My heart sank, as I was unsure if I had the ability to care and be responsible for another pet. (I had two cats and two of my sister's dogs lived with us.) I left the pet store, but that dog did not leave my mind.

I returned to the store a few hours later to view my new friend once again. As I approached the window, her tail began wagging and again she was looking at me, eyes wide open and body wiggling from the wagging of her tail. I decided it was fate. As we sat in the small "dog room", where I would sign the papers of purchase, this little white ball of fuzz raced incessantly around the chairs, grunting as she maneuvered the sharpest of turns. She would stop momentarily to jump up at me, and then continue her race. I remember thinking, "Uh-oh. I think I may be getting into more than I can handle." But it was too late, she was mine, and we left the store together.

And that's how it remained – together forever. She went everywhere with me. We went to dog shows and training classes. She loved to perform her repertoire of tricks, and loved applause as she would proudly prance like a horse at its inception. She was a therapy dog, and helped to start a local visiting schedule at various nursing homes. Shanna loved people, other animals, and me. We were inseparable, and she was, my very best friend.

Shanna was always happy. An occasional scolding would bring her down momentarily, but she would recover quickly with a toy or a "lick" attack. I could never stay upset with her for very long, she wouldn't allow it. She knew when I didn't feel well, and would stay by my side, even refusing food. If I had a "bad day", she would try anything to gain and sustain my attention, and it always worked!

As Shanna approached her thirteenth year of life, she began to have frequent bladder infections. After two courses of antibiotics, we decided to explore further possible causes. I never expected to hear or learn the outcome of her tests. Transitional cell carcinoma of the bladder was the formal diagnosis, and it was not a good prognosis. With treatment, most do not survive the year depending on the stage at diagnosis. I was heartbroken and devastated. How could my precious happy little friend be starting down the road to a grave illness? She didn't look or act ill. She showed no signs of pain or discomfort, initially. But the diagnosis was a fact – she would probably die.

Shanna had surgery on her bladder to remove the tumor, in hopes of staving off the inevitable for some time. She did well with the surgery, as Shanna was Shanna. Adversity did not have an impact on her; she continued living as though the fifteen sutures in her belly were nonexistent. Shanna remained happy even as she was led down the hospital hallway for yet another blood test or x-ray. The technicians and veterinarians loved her. She would frequently wag her tail and croon her hello upon seeing them. She would lick their hands as if to console them as they were placing the needle in her vein. When she had to be hospitalized, I went to visit her everyday. (The clinic was 35 miles away.) I had to see her, and I knew she had to see me. On one visit, the technician and I wanted to try an experiment. We decided that the technician would go into the hospital ward and observe Shanna to see how long it took her to recognize I was coming to see her. The technician was amazed and noted at the very second I entered the long hallway to the ward, Shanna's head immediately perked, and she began sniffing the air. As I came closer, she began jumping and crooning, this was behind a closed door.

She caught my scent and felt my presence long before I appeared. Everyone was amazed at the connections that this dog made.

We began cisplantin chemotherapy which was very rough on her body. I placed a red bandana around her neck, like some chemotherapy patients wear. Shanna thought this was cool, and proudly entered the vet's office with a bellowing croon to announce her arrival. Of course they all made a fuss. I fought back my tears as I left her there. We did not know what the outcome would be, but we had to try.

Throughout the course of Shanna's illness and treatments, I always tried to maintain a positive demeanor when I was with her. I did not speak of her illness around her, but would tell her of pending treatments or trips we would have to make. Some may think this was silly, but this dog understood so much language it was uncanny. I felt if she thought I was giving up, she would too. So, I requested that no one speak of the seriousness of her illness around her. I didn't want her to have any negative feelings for the road ahead, as she would need (as would I) all the courage and strength to contend with the future. Mid-way through chemotherapy, she became very depressed and lethargic. This was the first time I ever saw her lose her spunk and tenacity. A trip to the vet was warranted. The diagnosis was pancreatitis. She was very ill.

Within a few days of treatment she was back to her "old self" once again. She was running and playing with her other best friend Brenna, a Scottish terrier. It seemed as if nothing had ever happened. She was happy, and it filled my heart to watch her live once again. Chemotherapy had to be stopped, as obviously her system could not tolerate it. There were no other treatments. The inevitable waiting and watching would begin. During the late spring of her thirteenth year, I found a lump on her belly. Alarmed I immediately called the vet and took her for a visit. More bad news. She had developed a mammary tumor, and it would have to be removed as they are frequently malignant. I was warned that mammary cancer was frequently metastatic. Shanna had the surgery, and of course, it was malignant. I lamented inside questioning why this precious friend was being struck with yet another dismal malady. But I had to go on, for Shanna.

Brenna, my mother, and I brought Shanna home after her mammary surgery. This little white dog of fourteen pounds was sutured from her chest to the end of her belly. I believe there were 48 stitches. Shanna did not flinch or miss a beat. She was happy and playful, and was back to life. She amazed me with her spirit, and I envied her tenacity. I remember wishing I could be like her, and face what is given with courage and strength and a zest for life itself. A friend had stopped by soon after her surgery, and was amazed when I showed her Shanna's belly full of sutures. She could not believe that this dog was still so welcoming and happy. My friend thought we didn't have the surgery, because Shanna was so full of life. Again, at someone else's observance, I too was amazed at this little dog.

A few weeks later I discovered a little lump, on the edge of one of her bladder surgical scars. The report was not good. She had developed subcutaneous cancer on the incision. Based on all of her maladies, surgery or treatment was not an option at this point. It was felt she would not do well with any type of possible treatments. One more blow, in the life of this wonderful creature. I was becoming numb from the inevitable. I felt there was no hope except to fill her life with love, and soak up all she had to share. And we did!

By the end of May, Shanna was healing from her mammary cancer surgery and I decided to take a "special" vacation day, just to spend it with "my girls," Shanna and Brenna. We spent the day basking in the sun, planting flowers, and wading in the small pool. This day was almost spiritual for me. I felt more of a connection with my two friends, than ever before. Both of them would look at me in a way as if they were trying to relay a message, of hope, of love, of connection. I could not discern if my thoughts were self imposed, or if perhaps the "connections" were a reality. It really didn't matter as I reveled in those feelings; I felt hope and love abounding within my being.

A few days after our glorious special day, Shanna began to change. Sometimes she would sit and stare off into space, but responded quickly to my voice with a wag of her tail, and a "smooch." There were times when she seemed to be in pain, as she would tremble ever so slightly, but would calm somewhat when I held her. Eating became inconsistent. I felt time with my friend was slipping away, and there was nothing I could to do save her. But she saved me in more ways than ever imaginable! She spared me from showing overtly her illness. She remained happy and loving and attentive right up to the very end. She taught me to live, believe, embrace inner strength, and be happy in the moment.

As Shanna loved people and attention, I decided to have an "almost fourteen" birthday party for her. I decorated the deck with her newspaper clippings, as she was frequently photographed at local dog events. I got a cake and balloons, and invited a few friends and relatives with their dogs. Shanna, realizing "something" was happening out on the deck could hardly contain her excitement as she barked and paced in front of me. But I would not let her out until everyone arrived, as I wanted it to be a real surprise! When everyone finally arrived, I opened the door for my girl, and as everyone yelled "surprise", she spun around barking and crooning and vivaciously wagging her tail. She went to each person, on her own, and greeted them personally. I swore this dog was human, and had such a wonderful persona. She enjoyed her company and party, and was overtly happy throughout. When the party concluded, Shanna lay on the picnic table with her party hat askew, exhausted. But she enjoyed the day, and I was happy she had such fun.

Within a few days, Shanna began to deteriorate. Her appetite began to wane, she seemed to have difficulty breathing, and she sat more frequently. She continued to follow me every where and I almost felt guilty when I moved, as I knew she was uncomfortable. She still wagged her tail, and crooned when I spoke to her, but I could see she was becoming more distressed, and weak.

Shanna did not like thunderstorms, and that summer we had them in abundance. I had purchased an air conditioner to ease the stress of the summer heat and humidity on both the dogs, and my mother and me. During one particularly violent storm we lost electricity, and Shanna began to have more difficulty breathing. I placed her in my car, and we rode around town for two and one half hours until the electricity came back on. I actually relished this time with her, as I knew time was disappearing. She loved to ride in the car, but she could not rest during this ride. I stopped at a fast food restaurant to buy her a hamburger in hopes she would eat, but she only managed one bite. We finally returned home to electricity.

Neither of us could sleep that night, as Shanna seemed to not want to lie down. She would just sit on the bed and stare at me. She would snuggle at my request momentarily, but then discomfort would overcome her, and she would go back to sitting and watching me. I was overridden with guilt and anguish in my thoughts of what to do for her. Realistically, I knew the time had come, but from my heart I couldn't let go. I tormented and chastised myself for being so selfish. I was exhausted, heartbroken and distressed as I placed the call to the veterinarian's office. It was twelve midnight. Brenna, Shanna, my mother, and myself loaded ourselves in the car for the emotionally heart wrenching 35 mile drive to the vet's office. Shanna stood in the middle of the front seats, maneuvering every turn with assured balance, as always. She even sang with me to an "oldie" on the radio, as she frequently did when "we" were driving. I had to stop in the middle of the song, as I became "choked up" with emotion. I still didn't want to cry in front of her. I wept silently. She looked at me in question, touching her nose to mine, as she did so often. My consolation, she knew.

The doctor was waiting for us as we arrived. Shanna leaped out of the car crooning hello to the doctor and wagging her tail. I secretly prayed that this was not the end, and that the doctor would be able to provide some comfort. As the doctor examined her, her eyes filled with tears. I covered Shanna's ears, as I had done so often so she wouldn't hear negative statements. The doctor explained that there was barely any air going through her lungs, it was time. The most emotional moment in my life came barreling in at that second. We both tried to fight back tears as Shanna wagged her tail in my arms. The doctor asked me if I was ready.

I nodded, and held onto my girl, telling her I loved her. Within moments she slumped in my arms, and I cried like a baby. I told her I was sorry, as I sobbed hysterically. I held her and loved her for the final time.

I cried for six months, especially when it was time for bed, as she and Brenna were always in the bed with me. I missed her next to me. Brenna missed her too, as from that point on she never slept on the bed again. She would not stay; she slept on the floor at the bottom of the bed. Brenna was in mourning as she and Shanna were inseparable. The neighbors would tell me how Brenna would cry during the day. She was lonely and missed her friend. Brenna and I frequently visited Shanna's grave at the cemetery, and Brenna would just sit and stare. I wondered what she really thought, but I knew she missed her friend.

Life for Brenna and I was one of loss and grieving. Shanna was not around the corner, she was gone. I can truthfully say I was probably clinically depressed at losing my friend. But during this time I also had several revelations within myself. I had a renewal of spirit and hope as I contemplated what this little white dog gave me, through her spirit, courage, and devotion. She was an extraordinary teacher, and she showed me how to love and live unconditionally. Shanna taught me to look for the positive, because being positive eases the burdens of today, and tomorrow. A bright spot is always radiated, when I think of her. It is visual, I can see it, but most of all I can feel it. Shanna had a power, a strength, and fortitude. She was a gift and blessing from God. I am forever grateful for her, and one day hope to see her again.

During the months following Shanna's death, Brenna began to fall ill. Once again we began our search for a cause and hopefully, treatment. She was hospitalized off and on for several weeks, having biopsies, x-rays, and other diagnostics, but nothing definitive presented. Finally at a point of no return, the doctor requested to perform an exploratory surgery. Reluctantly I consented. As I waited in the waiting room during her surgery, I was summoned to the OR. The doctor told me she was full of cancer, the needle biopsies had missed the exact spots. There was no hope for recovery. As I held her in my arms while she remained under anesthesia, the doctor injected her. She died in my arms. Shanna and Brenna were together again. This time, forever. I lost my friends within six months of each other. My house, and my heart, was empty. The gifts I received live within me today. I cherish their memory, and hold them close in my heart. I never thought that I would learn, from my pets. But I did.

I tell my friends, "People can learn a lot from a dog," and I smile as I think of "my girls."

Author's Bio: Dana Smith-Mansell lives amid nature at the base of a mountain in Pennsylvania, residing with her husband and pets. Dana began writing poetry in the aftermath of September 11, 2001, as she discovered an avenue of hidden expression that guided her into writing poetry, essays, children's books, and fiction and non-fiction shorts. She has a Bachelor's Degree in Special Education, a Master's Degree in Behavior Disorders, and has focused her professional career on working with preschoolers with special needs and their families. Dana has volunteered for Hospice, and participates in Scottish and West Highland Terrier Rescue. She is an avid admirer and observer of nature, animals, and people.

SOARING WITH EAGLES

By Avis Townsend

When Mrs. Eagle was murdered, it became the talk of the town. Surprising the farmhand who was literally robbing her cookie jar, she picked up the baseball bat she'd kept for security and began swinging it at him. But the eighty-five-year-old woman was no match for the thirty-something handyman. He grabbed the bat from her and threw her to the floor. Before she could rise up, he bound her wrists and ankles with bridle reins, reins used on horses she had loved all her life, and he carried her to his car where he dumped her in the trunk.

Scared, and with adrenalin pumping through his veins, he drove to a nearby bridge, pulled over to the side, and threw her into the water. The fast moving current carried the terrified woman to the brink of a dam, where she was carried over a steep falls and pounded unmercifully into the rocks at the bottom. Eventually, her lifeless body escaped the water's torrent; and it drifted slowly north, where the creek trickled into the harbor and the entrance to Lake Ontario.

Her nightgown snagged upon a buoy, and they found her three days later, eyes still open, registering her shock and horror. The farmhand confessed when police came to the house. It was an easy case to solve. But it wasn't the end of the saga.

Mrs. Eagle was a miserable woman. She'd put two husbands in the ground without much display of grief. But she showered her love on her horses. She'd discovered American Saddlebreds when she was young, and she devoted her life to raising the most majestic, colorful specimens she could breed.

Never trusting anyone to care for them as she did, Mrs. Eagle was the sole handler. Every spring, she slept in the barn until all the mares foaled. She nurtured them when they were ill. She held their heads when the farrier worked on their feet, and she watched when the vets tended to them, lest the doctors made a mistake.

As she grew older, it was more difficult to handle the barn chores, so she hired various farmhands to clean the stalls, haul the hay, and do the mundane chores that didn't involve hands-on care for her creatures.

But she paid little and showed no mercy when her workers became ill or wanted vacation time. So, they came and went, but she didn't care. She just needed the labor and anyone could do it. If they left, they left. So be it, she thought.

However, she wasn't careful when she hired Tony Cushman [name has been changed for legal reasons]. She had long-since given up checking references, and the guy was bad news. After she'd turned down his request for higher wages, he decided to take them himself, and when she caught him in the act, he snapped.

It was months before anything was done about the horses. Neighbors came and fed them, but that was about all. No one cleaned the stalls, no one let them out to run. Their coats became dull, their heads drooped, and the once-proud animals became nags destined for the meat packers.

Mrs. Eagle had no friends or family, and the state was the sole beneficiary of her estate. Lawyers were hired to liquidate everything, and horses went to the highest bidder. Some went for use at riding stables. Some were sold to meat buyers.

Monty's Flying Eagle, the proudest stallion in the stable, was purchased by my neighbors, Jim and Lois Littles [names also fictional]. Monty had another chance at greatness, and a possibility of passing his great genes down and beginning a whole new line of horses.

When the Littles' brought him home, we all stood around and watched as he was led down from the trailer. Nostrils flaring, tail held high, he was still a beautiful sight, even though he was down three hundred pounds and his coat was dirty. When he was let into the pasture, however, he underwent a magnificent metamorphosis. It was as if the dirt disappeared. His coat glistened, the color of a freshly-minted penny. And like the coin, his copper color reflecting in the sunlight was bright enough to make one squint. He pranced around the pasture like he had always lived there, shaking his head, daring anyone to come in and try to slow him down.

For the first few days, people would pull off to the side of the road in their cars, reveling in the beauty of him. He was a sight to behold as he strutted his stuff, snorting and kicking up dirt. He seemed to know he was one of earth's most beautiful creatures.

Within a week, however, he was very ill. The Littles, unaware that a tiny scratch to the foot could cause tetanus, avoided getting the shots needed when transporting a new horse from one farm to the next. It was a simple, but costly, mistake.

At first Monty became sullen, head lowered, ears to the side, not wanting to eat. The vet was called and immediately diagnosed tetanus. He injected the horse with an antitoxin, but it was too late. The next day Monty was down, moaning as he lay on his side, and by the following day he was dead. The Littles' had to knock a stall wall out to get a tractor in and drag him out. They buried him in back of their apple orchard. He would never run again, never produce an heir to carry the Eagle heritage.

It's been many years since Monty's death, but I will always remember him vividly. I still search for a horse as magnificent, but I have never found one. I have resigned myself to know that I will never see the brilliant copper that gleamed in the sun, nor will I ever see a horse as proud or majestic as Monty's Flying Eagle.

SURPRISE IN THE HENHOUSE

By Barbara Williamson-Wood

I raise many breeds of chickens - Rhode Island Reds, Bantams, and Barred Rock to name a few. Nothing is more precious, as well as amusing, than to watch the hens as their chicks hatch.

We have all heard stories about dogs nursing kittens or vice versa. So it makes sense to pass eggs from one hen to the other to incubate and hatch, especially when one makes a better mother than another.

I have a Barred Rock hen. For those who are unfamiliar with this breed, I will describe them to you. A Barred Rock chicken weighs about 5 to six pounds, with black and white stripes throughout their feathers, thus the title "barred." They are rather big in size and normally very good egg layers.

This particular hen had not been laying for some time, however, although she still would try to "sit" anywhere. It did not matter to her if she had eggs under her or not. If I put apples under her she probably would have continued to sit. I guess she figured if she sat long enough (which is 21 days for chickens) something would happen.

Feeling sorry for her I put some eggs under her that I had gathered. Some were from the Bantam breed, which is small, getting top weight at about 2 pounds. I also put some of the Rhode Island eggs under her. They can get as heavy as 12 pounds.

The hen felt content sitting there day after day. I marked off twenty-one days on the calendar and waited along with her in anticipation. When the day arrived I went to check on her and heard the familiar peep-peep.

Out from under Mama's wing came a little baby chick. He was a Bantam - cute as a button and as small as one too, considering who his new Mama was and the breed he was. It was a sight, but even funnier was his little brother who hatched out after him a few hours later. Little brother was a Rhode Island Red chick. His bright red feathers were in contrast to Mama's black and white zebra markings. Also his size in comparison to the hen and his "older" brother's little size just made me laugh at the sight of them. No other eggs hatched, only the two.

It was the strangest thing to look at all three of them. There were Big Mama and her two very different children. Mama hen didn't care. Those were her babies and she loved them and fought to protect them from any harm from the rest of the other meddling hens.

Looking into the pen this morning as I was throwing out some scratch, I was reminded of how much this hen and her chicks were like many human families. We are all different, different looks with different size and colors. That is why Mamas are very special. They love you for what and who you are...for being you.

Author's Bio: Barbara Williamson-Wood, a freelance writer and author, enjoys writing and reminiscing of her life growing up in the mountains. Her first book, *Through My Eyes*, is a collection of short stories, essays and verse. Her second book, *Inner Trappings,* is a suspense thriller for which she is currently seeking publication. Her work is showcased at her website http://windwalker32113_1.tripod.com/ .

TALKING SOFTLY WITH AN EQUINE BEST FRIEND

By Tricia Draper

"Why do you even bother talking to them? They are horses. They don't understand your words. They learn by teaching, not by just talking."

I have heard that all my life. I grew up around horses. At three days old, I had my first ride, and I've been hooked ever since. My great-grandfather owned a riding stable in Des Moines, IA. People of all ages came to take trail rides through the hills, trees, creeks, everything. We had hayrides, bon fires, and best of all, family reunions. We moved to Texas when I was 6, but every summer I went up to stay with my grandparents. When we were old enough, my cousins and I would lead the trails, just as my father had done before me.

When I was in fifth grade, Dad told me there was a horse in Iowa that would be mine. We had horses in Texas, but not one of my own. We went to get the yearling, but we found she had a hernia. This wasn't a rare occasion, and it's usually fine after being removed. However, in this case, there were complications. Her name was Mattie's Medallion, and we called M&M, because it's my favorite candy. All I could do was hold her head in my lap and pet her over and over as the tears fell from my face to her cheek. I spoke softly as she passed away, cradled in my lap as a baby. It was the first day I'd ever seen her, but she was my baby, if only for a few hours.

I got Mattie's newest foal, and I named her Mattie's 2nd Medallion, or M2M. Eventually it went to M&M. Every day I went to see her. We were soul mates instantly. After a few days, she'd walk up to me, let me put on a halter, and follow me everywhere I went. She and I talked about everything. Well, I did most of the talking, but she was a great listener. As I slipped off the halter after each session, I gave her hugs, and soon she returned them.

We brought her back to Texas, and she was tamer than the other horses we'd had for years. She learned to listen and obey me. My father has trained horses since he was a boy, but our relationship still baffles his mind. For example, one day my dad was trying to clip her hooves. He'd done this with horses for 25 years, but he was having a hard time with her. I turned and said, "M&M, lift your foot, please." You should have seen the absolute shock on my father's face as she simply lifted the foot he wanted. When I put her halter on, I just let the rope hang over my shoulder. Even today, if she's in a big pasture, all I have to do is call her name, and she comes running.

She is now about 15-years old. We've been through good times and bad. No matter what happens, I can always talk to her. I've talked her through sickness, and she talked me through my rough pregnancy. We were both pregnant and miserable, and it was wonderful to have something so special in common with her.

Her hugs are the absolute best, and her kisses are sweet as honey. You doubt? How can a horse kiss, you ask? Very easily, with her head nestled on my shoulder, and her heart shining through her eyes.

Tricia Draper's author's bio has been listed in her other story, *A Place for Kitty.*

THE COLONY

By Debora Hill

By the time he died in March of 2003, nobody knew just how old Mr. Nick was. He was the patriarch of the group when Emily found him, cast off by some uncaring owner. He was already an old cat. At his death he was somewhere between fifteen and twenty, probably closer to the latter than the former. When I bought the little green cottage in May of 2000, I didn't know about the cat colony. I had one cat of my own, Miss Gidget, a spoiled princess who considered herself above most other felines. She'd had a rough couple of years; first she lost her long-time companion Marbles, an elderly gentleman part-Siamese many years older than she. Then my mother, her second-best human friend, died, and she was left with only me.

The green cottage is in a planned development like nothing else in Sonoma County, California. A semi-circle of little detached houses that resemble Pennsylvania Dutch farmhouses, Windmill Farms is surrounded by parkland and trees – a cat haven. There is only one road in, and that dead-ends when the houses end, so there is nowhere for cars to go; that means not many people come into the Farms, even with 100 houses on the enormous property.

Three days after Miss Gidget and I moved into what my friends dubbed 'Debora's Dollhouse', another cat appeared in my back garden and was disinclined to leave. She was a beautiful big calico, obviously well-fed and cared for, but now she was sleeping on my porch swing. I asked my new neighbors and discovered that her name was ChuCha, and she belonged to Doris and George, who lived in a yellow house a few doors down. They had allowed their son, who appeared to be 21-going on-10, to bring home a black Labrador puppy, and ChuCha decided to exit the premises. She refused to even allow Doris near her. I had a second cat.

Unfortunately, ChuCha (whom I renamed Chewbacca after I saw her eat) and Miss Gidget hated one another on sight. This was ok during the warm months, of which there are many in California, but what would happen once the rains started? Chewie solved this problem herself — when I covered the porch swing with a blue tarp for the winter, Chewie decided it was now her tent. It still is, complete with comforter and pillow.

I learned about The Colony during my second week in residence. My neighbor across the lane (there are no streets in Windmill Farms apart from the access road, only tree-lined lanes) is named Emily, and she volunteers with Forgotten Felines, a feral cat rescue organization. And despite being allergic to cats, Emily is the custodian of a colony of feral cats who live in Windmill Farms. Nick was the patriarch of the colony, and his death left his best friend, Little Gingerman, bereft and lonely. Nick was a big black-and-white, an alpha male who was the official greeter in my little corner of the Farms. He befriended everyone, and perched on the cars of visitors who were leaving, refusing to budge until they petted him. He was very affectionate and outgoing, a real character. At first, I helped with the colony by buying bags of kibble for Emily. I became friends with Nick, Little Gingerman, Midnight Louie (thanks to Carole Nelson Douglas, originator of the original big black cat of that name), Kevin and a few other members of the colony. Some of the members I've never seen after three years at the Farm; they never became acclimated to people and have spent their whole lives feral. But the regulars have become my charge as well as Emily's; I feed them in the morning and she feeds them at night.

Nick was a healthy old man who refused to be indoors because he couldn't remember ever living in a house. Emily has baskets underneath the ledge in the front of her house, protected by a Plexiglas shield. But one day during the summer of 2002 he started to lie in my front yard, staying there all night. I didn't notice at first, but my neighbor Carrie did, and she brought him over a laundry basket with a fluffy pad inside. Then Emily gave me two kitty heating pads; one for the basket and one for Chewie's tent. They look like fat pink Frisbees; you put them in the microwave for six or seven minutes and they stay warm all night long. I put a quilt into the basket and the heating pad went under the top of the quilt. But Nick could still get wet during the rain; I solved this with a little umbrella — a giveaway from the Humane Society, which I thought was appropriate. It shields the front of the basket and keeps the basket and bedding dry. On cold nights Nick and Little Gingerman would be in the basket together, best friends who kept one another warm and shared the sleeping pad.

In the autumn of 2002 a new kitten showed up in the colony. A tiny, all black baby who was too afraid to allow any of us to get close to him. But he knew I fed the cats every morning; Carrie made him a bed in front of her house similar to the one I had for Nick, and every morning I would take Peanut (Emily named him) his own little bowl of food. He still hasn't let me pet him, but he runs to me if I call.

In early March, Nick wasn't doing well. Emily took him to the vet and it turned out he needed oral surgery to remove some teeth. But after he returned home, he never recovered. For a week, he hardly ate anything. When Emily returned him to the vet, they did some tests and discovered Nick was suffering from kidney failure. He had to be put to sleep.

A few weeks later, Little Gingerman is still searching for his best friend. He has taken over Nick's basket and sleeps there every night. He and Peanut have become friends; it hasn't yet made up for the loss of Nick, but the colony continues and we, their human friends, help them as best we can. They were all castoffs, unwanted and unneeded, but in this place, they have found a haven.

In August of 2003, my assistant brought me a tiny kitten who was in terrible shape. She and her sister rescued him from the backyard of a woman who flung him out there at four weeks old to fend for himself. He was emaciated, had ear mites, fleas and worms. He is now named Shadow Hawke, after the film company we work with in Ireland, and at six months old he weighed 7.5 pounds. Peanut has become his best friend, but he's already bigger than his friend, who is a year older. He loves Windmill Farms and all the feral cats are his friends. This place has become his haven as well.

Author's Bio: Debora Hill was born in San Francisco in 1961, and still lives in Northern California in a little green cottage with three cats—Miss Gidget, Chewbacca and Shadow Hawke. She has published three nonfiction books about music and two novels. Her third novel, *A WIZARD BY ANY OTHER NAME*, has been taken for publication. "I have worked as a rock music journalist, a fine arts interviewer and reporter, and an investigative journalist. Currently I am working film and have a three-picture production deal with Shadow Hawk Productions (Ireland) and United Film International."

THE PILSBURY DOUGH DOG

Internet Joke That's Made the Rounds

We have a fox terrier by the name of Jasper. He came to us in the summer of 2001 from the fox terrier rescue program. For those of you who are unfamiliar with this type of adoption, imagine taking in a 10-year-old child whom you know nothing about and committing to doing your best to be a good parent. Like the child, the dog came with his own idiosyncrasies. He will only sleep on the bed, on top of the covers, nuzzled as close to my face as he can get without actually performing a French kiss on me. Lest you think this is a bad case of no discipline, I should tell you that Perry and I tried every means to break him of this habit including locking him in a separate bedroom for several nights. The new door cost over $200.

But I digress. Five weeks ago we began remodeling our house. Although the cost of the project is downright obnoxious, it was 20 years overdue AND it got me out of cooking Thanksgiving for family, extended family and a lot of drunk friends that I like more than family most of the time. I was however assigned the task of preparing 124 of my famous yeast dinner rolls for the two Thanksgiving feasts we did attend. I am still cursing the electrician for getting the new oven hooked up so quickly. It was the only appliance in the whole damn house that worked thus the assignment.

I made the decision to cook the rolls on Wednesday evening to reheat on Thursday morning. Since the kitchen was freshly painted you can imagine the odor. Not wanting the rolls to smell like Sherwin Williams latex paint #586, I put the rolls on baking sheets and set them in the living room to rise for 5 hours. After 3 hours, Perry and I decided to go out to eat, returning in about an hour. An hour later the rolls were ready to go in the oven. It was 8:30pm. When I went to the living room to retrieve the pans, much to my shock one whole pan of 12 rolls was empty. I called out to Jasper and my worst nightmare became a reality. He literally wobbled over to me. He looked like a combination of the Pillsbury dough boy and the Michelin Tire man wrapped up in fur. He groaned when he walked. I swear even his cheeks were bloated.

I ran to the phone and called our vet. After a few seconds of uproarious laughter, he told me the dog would probably be OK however I needed to give him Pepto Bismol every 2 hours for the rest of the night. God only knows why I thought a dog would like Pepto Bismol any more than my kids did when they were sick. Suffice to say that by the time we went to bed the dog was black, white and pink. He was so bloated we had to lift him onto the bed for the night. Naively thinking the dog would be all better by morning was very stupid on my part. We arose at 7:30 and as we always do first thing; put the dogs out to relieve themselves. Well, the damn dog was as drunk as a sailor on his first leave. He was running into walls, falling flat on his butt and most of the time when he was walking his front half was going one direction and the other half was either dragging the floor or headed 90 degrees in another direction. He couldn't lift his leg to pee so he would just walk and pee at the same time. When he ran down the small incline in our back yard he couldn't stop himself and nearly ended up running into the fence. His pupils were dilated and he was as dizzy as a loon. I endured another few seconds of laughter from the vet (second call within 12 hours) before he explained that the yeast had fermented in his belly and that he was indeed drunk. He assured me that, not unlike most binges we humans go through, it would wear off after about 4 or 5 hours and to keep giving him Pepto Bismol.

Afraid to leave him by himself in the house, Perry and I loaded him up and took him with us to my sister's house for the first Thanksgiving meal of the day. My sister lives outside of Muskogee on a ranch (10 to 15 minute drive).Rolls firmly secured in the trunk (124 less 12) and drunk dog leaning from the back seat onto the console of the car between Perry and I, we took off. Now I know you probably don't believe that dogs burp, but believe me when I say that after eating a tray of risen unbaked yeast rolls, DOGS WILL BURP. These burps were pure Old Charter. They would have matched or beat any smell in a drunk tank at the police station. But that's not the worst of it. Now he was beginning to fart and they smelled like baked rolls. God strike me dead if I am not telling the truth! We endured this for the entire trip to Karee's, thankful she didn't live any further away than she did.

Once Jasper was firmly placed in her garage with the door locked, we finally sat down to enjoy our first Thanksgiving meal of the day. The dog was the topic of conversation all morning long and everyone made trips to the garage to witness my drunk dog, each returning with a tale of Jasper's latest endeavor to walk without running into something.

Of course, as the old adage goes, "what goes in must come out" and Jasper was no exception. Granted if it had been me that had eaten 12 risen unbaked yeast rolls you might as well have put a concrete block up my ass but alas a dog's digestive system is quite different from yours or mine. I discovered this was a mixed blessing when we prepared to leave Karee's house. Having discovered his "packages" on the garage floor, we loaded him up in the car so we could hose down the floor. This was another naive decision on our part. The blast of water from the hose hit the shit on the floor and the shit on the floor withstood the blast from the hose. It was like Portland cement beginning to set up and cure. We finally resorted to scooping it up with a shovel. I (obviously no one else was going to offer their services) had to get on my hands and knees with a coarse brush to get the remnants off of the floor. And as if this wasn't degrading enough, the damn dog in his drunken state had walked through the poop and left paw prints all over the garage floor that had to be brushed too.

Well, by this time the dog was sobering up nicely so we took him home and dropped him off before we left for our second Thanksgiving dinner at Perry's sister's house. I am happy to report that as of today (Monday) the dog is back to normal both in size and temperament. He has had a bath and is no longer tricolor. Nonetheless for wear I presume. I am also happy to report that just this evening I found 2 risen unbaked yeast rolls hidden inside my closet door. It appears he must have come to his senses after eating 10 of them but decided hiding 2 of them for later would not be a bad idea. If any of you have a suggestion as to how I can remove unbaked dough from carpeting I would certainly appreciate your feedback!

THE RETRIEVAL

By Tova Gabrielle

During a week of camping in Northern California, I unknowingly contracted Lyme disease. On the plane ride home, I felt like a sudden case of flu was upon me, and over the next couple of weeks it flared up into something much worse.

One of my symptoms was depression. For weeks, I lay in bed, and between the muscle relaxants, pain killers, and antibiotics, I found myself obsessing about a comment my neighbor had made to me months ago when he saw my exotic birds: "I'd like to kill birds-as hobby, that is... Can't stand 'em."

How was I to deal with someone whose basic philosophy (he's an exterminator) seems to be, "if it moves, kill it"? How was I to deal with finding that the general (and formerly avoidable) evil in the world was now living next door to me?

I am a freak for meaning. It is the only thing that makes suffering bearable. In illness one can find ample lessons. With the onset of Lyme disease and then the loss I was about to experience, I was forced to admit that even I have limits.

My story begins on a Thursday afternoon on the deck outside of my condo, where I was just lifting my rare Red Fronted Macaw, Ruby, from her cage. Ruby gingerly stepped onto the stick I held to her chest. Although her flight feathers were clipped, she bolted and soared up into the woods behind my house. She was gone as unpredictably as she'd come to me, just a week or so before....

Ruby and her mate, Rudy, had been given to me by Jean, an animal lover I'd met when retrieving my sixteen-year old son, Julian, from her house. At that time, I'd heard her birds calling from inside and asked to see them because I worked with birds. Jean told me how frustrated she was with their screaming as she eagerly led me into a back room where her two birds had sat for ten years and had not mated in spite of her following all the recommendations. I was captivated by their two-and-a-half-feet-long green bodies, bright red heads, and the orange and blue markings on their wings. But when Rudy sidled up to me at the side of his cage, gave a soft appreciative little whistle, and then whispered to me, "Hi, how are you...?" I was almost giddy with delight. ly even thought I'dsliped her.

Breeders say that if you want birds to mate, give them a very large cage and leave them alone. I guess as with humans, desperation breeds affection. The only problem is that birds fall in lust with the objects they first see when they open their eyes, and since these birds were hand fed, that spelled trouble in the nesting box.

For a decade, Ruby and Rudy had tried to woo Jean and her husband, Harry, who, being the strong man he was, was less taken in by their ruses. Dear Jean had been more seduced and consequently more hurt. She had learned fear the hard way at the end their enormous beaks. Once, Rudy, probably frustrated by too much time in that back room and over-zealous to be out, had bitten her hand, and the wound required stitches. Since then, she'd left the beasts to abuse each other. Sigh. Such is the way of family dynamics.

Macho Woman that I was, I remained un-phased by this news. I wanted those darlings, and if I got hurt, well, it wouldn't have been the first time. Common sense is always the first thing to flee from me in new affairs of the heart.

For the next hour, Jean and Harry watched me work with the birds as the birds worked on me. I began by establishing who's who in the pecking order. With the constraints of a stick and towel, I taught them to step up onto the stick. Rudy tried to nip me but stopped himself yelling, "Ouch! Bad bird!" in Jean's voice. I encouraged them to come to me and then to allow me to hold them. Although I haven't had much luck in love when asserting my dominance with homo-sapiens (particularly the males) birds are not too worried about their identities to respond-they KNOW they are flock animals. They learned to step up onto the stick, then nuzzle against my chest in the towel (now this trick is not difficult to teach homo-sapiens, but they tend to have trouble with the rest). Holding them close, they were reassured by the sounds of my heartbeat and reassuring words.

Jean asked me if I would consider taking them, even though she could sell them. She said she knew that I would make them happy. She would have visiting rights. I was sure I could get them to at least stop screaming and biting. Within a week they were adjusting well in my aviary, new members of the flock that included my Blue Front Amazon, Scarlet Collared Mini-Macaw, and two Goffins Cockatoos. Birds view their caretakers as part of their flock, and the newcomers soon made friends with my son, Julian, and my partner, Gary. I had clipped both birds at Jean's and it seemed they were very poor fliers indeed. (Now I see that they were just out of shape from not having been out of their cage for a decade).

Well, it's amazing what a lift the outdoors can give a being. I opened the cage and pushed a stick in front of Ruby. In her timid way, she reluctantly stepped onto it and then suddenly bolted into the woods behind my house. Now, that's scary. Parrots have extremely sensitive lungs and cannot easily survive in temperatures below fifty degrees if there is wind. Domestics didn't get their flight training as bappies (baby birds). They have an absolutely lousy sense of direction. But you would certainly think that landing on the ground would come naturally. Wrong. (Just think what it would be like to try to walk at age ten if you'd never learned.)

Ruby flew into the woods. I couldn't see her, but I could hear her whistling and calling Jean's husband's name ("Harry, Harry!"). I found her perched on the top of a huge oak tree. We whistled back and forth for most of the afternoon. By evening Ruby tried to fly to me but flew right over the house to the edge of the woods on the other side.

I thought that surely she'd come to me, then, because she was facing the house, and even if she landed on the roof she'd come down for food and warmth as evening set in. I put Rudy in a cage and plunked it outside (don't try this with humans). Rudy thought he knew just how to approach this, calmly calling, "Ruby, birdie, what's up; how are you?" Apparently now that she was footloose and free, she didn't have to listen to him. But rather than cheering for her like the feminist I think I am, I just watched with despair as she took off into woods that went down to a swamp and over to the dreaded Route 21. I didn't sleep well at all that night. Soon I would be nuts.

The next morning, Ruby mimicked my calls and whistles heartily, from somewhere in the woods that ended near another dreaded highway. Route

9 is a busy road that leads into the enormous Quabbin Reservoir. I knew if she crossed that road and I didn't retrieve her very soon, I'd lose her.

Perhaps you would think there is a difference between a human/bird bond and a human/human bond that would temper my attachment and fear of loss. There is; however, it didn't allay it: I get along better with birds.

All day I followed her, and by dusk she began screaming to me in desperation. She didn't know how to hunt, especially for water. Finally I caught up with her in the woods. I was feeling faint. By now, neighbors from four consecutive homes had come out and tried to help. They called to her, craned their necks, offered chaise lounges (to me, not Ruby) and camping equipment (for me or Ruby). They put out food on the ground.

An odd transformation was beginning: My bird had fled the coop but my faith in humanity was returning. It was like a mini national emergency. I called the police and the dog pound. The dog pound lady called me back and suggested I contact a tree climber.

Meanwhile, Ruby kept trying to fly to me and overshooting. Now the neighbors were the ones to track her back into the woods toward the Quabbin Reservoir.

I don't even recall if I slept that night.

The next day, fever and exhaustion convinced me to get more help. I called Canadian Tree Service. Bernie, the owner, said, "Hang in there." He was on his way with a bucket loader. He'd have to bring me up in the bucket with him and we'd surely get the job done. Within the hour, he arrived at Ruby's tree and when we were within ten feet of her, she bolted towards the Quabbin.

Back on Earth, I remained delirious. I was leaning on Gary and became dizzy; I fell on him and he fell onto a woodpile. Worst of all, he got mad about it. Well, I told Gary later, it's no wonder I'm an animal person. Fortunately, Annette, an empathetic neighbor, showed Gary a thing or two, rushing to my rescue with cold drinks and aspirin.

Now, maybe I should have dated Bill instead, whose yard abutted Annette's. Bill stayed outside a great deal of the weekend, tracking the bird, letting us use his bathroom, and offering food and water for the bird. On second thought, I probably should have just stayed with birds: Bill seemed married to his dear old mother. His mother was a nurse who worked the graveyard shift, but nonetheless she made sandwiches which he offered us. Bill put in many hours calling Ruby's name, after we left on those two endless days. The neighbors continued to come out of the woodwork.

People offered their driveways, ladders, and yards for our operation, as well as their own bird stories. I cried on one grandmotherly farmwoman's shoulder when she asked me what else I needed. All of them were caretakers of one sort or another – Annette worked in a home for disabled persons, Bill worked with a woman with Alzheimer's – and they all pitched in as if it were only natural, which it was. Yet how rare I'd believed such neighborly kindness to be, before Ruby took flight.

Because Ruby was flying so high and was not tame enough to grab or climb down to us, I was losing heart, not to mention energy.

My son Julian, had been through this before, although not so dramatically, when our Cockatoo flew into the woods. He knew I never gave up hope. And so when I said something he'd never heard me say in all his sixteen years – "I give up" – he simply looked at me blankly.

I went home and didn't sleep much that night, knowing the temperature was going down into the forties. I felt guilty closing the window. I lied to my son and said Ruby could easily adapt to the cold.

Before I hit the sack, I went on the Internet and opened a message, "Words of hope and healing". Rabbi Baruch had written that no matter what befalls us, people must never ever give up hope. There is always hope. Just before I fell asleep I had an image of Ruby and Rudy back together by the next day, but it didn't seem possible.

I lay awake, thinking of Ruby until 4:00 A.M. At 5:30 I headed over to the tall trees across the highway. I spotted her sleeping, all puffed up and with her head tucked into her back for warmth. I lugged Rudy back out and he called to her shrilly, but she answered meekly. It was obvious to me she was not well, although the neighbors insisted she was having a time of it with me. I knew better.

At 11:30 that Sunday morning I went back to the house while Bill and Annette watched for her and kept vigil on Rudy's cage. I told Julian again that I was giving up. He, however, cancelled going to work and insisted he could get her. I thought he was kidding himself saying grimly to him, "How do you catch a half tamed, flighted, frightened, confused bird?" He'd never heard me speak like this and wasn't about to believe me.

He went into the woods with a neighbor and they spotted her about 40 or 50 feet up in an evergreen. I fell asleep at last with a sinking feeling in my heart. About 45 minutes later the phone rang. I was out of it. When my son yelled, "I got her!" I was so discouraged I didn't know whom he'd gotten.

What did he mean? I'd asked; a girlfriend? Or what? And why couldn't it wait? "Her, Ruby, I got her!" he yelled breathlessly into the phone.

I jumped up and ran out to the car where I tried to zip over, fearing if I took too long I could learn she'd gotten away again. I had to sit for almost ten minutes as a virtual parade of motorcycles blocked my driveway.

When I finally crossed, I saw my son marching with a huge grin towards me, but – no bird. Then I realized she was tucked inside his sweatshirt. The neighbors all came out and raved about his bravery and said he'd accomplished the impossible. He'd climbed to the top of that enormous tree and with only his legs wrapped around the trunk, held out a stick with a piece of bagel on it. She'd leaned gingerly towards the bagel and he grabbed her leg. She didn't struggle.

I brought her home and she pressed her long body into my torso for warmth, no longer shy. Although I haven't seen any wild dancing between them, Rudy and Ruby have stayed close by each other, nuzzling and preening and mumbling happily.

One slight observation: When I first put Ruby on the kitchen counter with Rudy so that she could revive herself, she ate and drank so much she was coughing, and Rudy, typical of some humans I've known, kept pushing her out of his way so he could get more food. Perhaps that's the real reason she won't mate with him.

Author's Bio for Tova Gabrielle is included in her other story, *Clyde's Gift*.

TROUBLE

By Heide A.W. Kaminski

I took my 15-year-old dog to the veterinarian, and I did not bring her back home...

"Trouble" entered my life, when she was only about 9 weeks old. My ex-husband brought her home two days after my first dog had died a tragic death. He couldn't stand my sorrow and decided getting a new puppy right away would ease my pain.

Trouble was very affectionate, but one thing she would never do: she never wanted to sleep on my bed with me. Beside the bed, yes, but on it - no way. When I eventually left my husband, I remember the very first night alone in the bed in my new apartment. I was crying myself to sleep, when suddenly Trouble snuggled up close to me. It was the only time in her life she ever got onto the bed with me.

Today, after many months of debating among the family members, I took her to be put to rest.

I cried so hard, the vet's assistant suggested I did not stay for the actual deed. As I was leaving the building, I could hear her distinctive howl. Fortunately I only had less than a mile to drive home. I felt like a murderer. If we would have had the chance last night to have her put to sleep, not a shred of doubt would have been in my mind. She was miserable. Today, she wandered around a bit, and she actually wagged her tail. That was something I hadn't seen her do in months! Thus doubts crept back into my head. Did I really have to? As I cried on the phone to the receptionist at the vet's, she assured me that sooner or later I would regret not having brought her in today.

When I got home, I dug a half-smoked cigarette out of the ashtray. I stood by the kitchen window, sucking on the butt, begging my dog for forgiveness.

Then it happened! A hummingbird approached my bush. It fluttered from flower to flower and then sat down and stopped fluttering. Hummingbirds rarely stop fluttering, so this was a special incident. It did this three times. Then it turned and looked at me for a few seconds, before he flew off. I was immediately overcome by a sense of serenity and I thanked God for sending me this sign. Months ago a highly spiritual friend of mine had told me that hummingbirds, who stop at your house and especially the ones that turn and look at you for a while, are angel messengers. It was clear that my dog had quickly stopped by to tell me that she was OK. I continued the day feeling sad, but I didn't need to cry anymore...

Author's Bio: Heide AW Kaminski is a single mother, newspaper reporter, frequent anthology contributor, spiritual newsletter feature's writer, online women's monthly newsletter creator, published author, writing contest entry queen and preschool art teacher in Tecumseh, Michigan. In between she dreams of becoming as rich and famous as her idol J.K. Rowling. Check out her newest book *Get Smart Through Art*, Datamaster Publishing, ISBN 0967088690 on www.amazon.com.

UGLY, THE RESIDENT TOM

Author Unknown

Everyone in the apartment complex I lived in knew who Ugly was. Ugly was the resident tomcat. Ugly loved three things in this world: fighting, eating garbage, and, shall we say, love, the combination of these things combined with a life spent outside had their effect on Ugly. To start with, he had only one eye and where the other should have been was a hole. He was also missing his ear on the same side. His left foot appeared to have been badly broken at one time and had healed at an unnatural angle, making him look like he was always turning the corner.

Ugly would have been a dark gray tabby, striped type, except for the sores covering his head, neck, and even his shoulders. Every time someone saw Ugly there was the same reaction. "That's one UGLY cat!!! All the children were warned not to touch him, the adults threw rocks at him, hosed him down, squirted him when he tried to come in their homes, or shut his paws in the door when he would not leave. Ugly always had the same reaction.

If you turned the hose on him, he would stand there, getting soaked until you gave up and quit. If you threw things at him, he would curl his lanky body around your feet in forgiveness. Whenever he spied children, he would come running, meowing frantically and bump his head against their hands, begging for their love. If you ever picked him up he would immediately begin suckling on your shirt, earrings, whatever he could find. One day Ugly shared his love with the neighbor's dogs. They did not respond kindly, and Ugly was badly mauled. I tried to rush to his aid. By the time I got to where he was laying, it was apparent Ugly's sad life was almost at an end. As I picked him up and tried to carry him home, I could hear him wheezing and gasping, and could feel him struggling. It must be hurting him terribly, I thought.

Then I felt a familiar tugging, sucking sensation on my ear. Ugly, in so much pain, suffering and obviously dying, was trying to suckle my ear. I pulled him closer to me, and he bumped the palm of my hand with his head, then he turned his one golden eye towards me, and I could hear the distinct sound of purring. Even in the greatest pain, that ugly battled scarred cat was asking only for a little affection, perhaps some compassion. At that moment I thought Ugly was the most beautiful, loving creature I had ever seen. Never once did he try to bite or scratch me, try to get away from me, or struggle in any way. Ugly just looked up at me completely trusting in me to relieve his pain. Ugly died in my arms before I could get inside, but I sat and held him for a long time afterwards, thinking about how one scarred, deformed little stray could so alter my opinion about what it means to have true pureness of spirit, to love so totally and truly. Ugly taught me more about giving and compassion than a thousand books, lectures, or talk show specials ever could, and for that I will always be thankful. He had been scarred on the outside, but I was scarred on the inside, and it was time for me to move on and learn to love truly and deeply. To give my total to those I cared for. Many people want to be richer, more successful, well liked, beautiful, popular, but for me... I will always try to be Ugly.

WAITING FOR MY BEST FRIEND

Author Unknown

I explained to St. Peter
I'd rather stay here
Outside the pearly gate.

I won't be a nuisance
I won't even bark
I'll be very patient and wait.

I'll be here chewing on a celestial bone
No matter how long you may be.
I'd miss you too much,
if I went in alone -
It just wouldn't be Heaven for me.

WHEN ROCKY BECAME ROXANNE

By Avis Townsend

When a full-grown raccoon decided to take up residence in our garage, I was more than a little concerned. With six dogs and a dozen cats, not to mention six horses grazing on the back forty, I was annoyed that the furry thing would take up residence in our garage, when he had so many outbuildings, wood piles, and hidden nooks and crannies to call home.

Also, harboring a raccoon in Western New York is a crime. Not only would health department officials come and kill the creature, but they could also slap you with a hefty fine if they wanted to.

When we first bought our place in 1995, the rabies epidemic was at its height. Farmers and hunters were especially scared, and they were told to shoot any raccoon in sight. I always felt bad about the situation, because I'd gone to high school with a girl who kept a pet raccoon, and she never had a problem. When they attended outdoor events together, the raccoon was either on a leash or perched upon its owner's neck, like a living stole.

All of a sudden the rabies scare hit, and raccoons were considered deadly.

A few years ago, however, various New York counties began the bait and drop program, a well-planned system of dropping foil-wrapped cubes into woodlands and meadows. Smelling like fish and colored bright yellow, they were designed to attract raccoons and other wildlife. The creatures would eat them and be immunized against rabies. Infected animals would die off, and the ones remaining would live rabies-free.

It worked. According to wildlife rehabilitator Kathy Britton, at least 95 percent of New York's raccoons are rabies-free as a result of the drop.

So, I didn't need to be afraid of our guest, but I didn't realize that at the time.

I discovered the raccoon on a Tuesday morning, as I was getting ready for work. I looked out my kitchen window and noticed the cats had gathered at the base of our large tree, staring up at something in the branches above. Thinking it was a family of birds, I went out to shoo the cats away, and saw the raccoon staring down at me. It was clicking and clucking, and making small squealing sounds, obviously concerned about being cornered by a bunch of cats.

I grabbed all the felines and put them in the house, then hit the base of the tree and said to the raccoon, "OK, you can come down now."

Imagine my shock when he did just that. Talking and clucking, he came down the branches like a pro, and started running toward me when he hit the ground.

"Rabies" was the first thing that entered my mind. I grabbed a lawn rake and put it in front of me, yelling at the beast to get away. He was undaunted. Not only did he follow me to the house, but when I ducked in and closed the door behind me, the raccoon began opening and closing the screen with his hands. Yes, I said hands.

Raccoons' paws are similar to humans, with individual fingers. This one was very adept at opening the door, like it had opened one before.

But, I managed to elude him that morning. Knowing it was getting late, I finished getting dressed for work, hoping the raccoon would be gone by the time it was ready to leave. However, he had other plans. When I left, he was back in the tree, climbing up and down the limbs, knocking the small ones off as he moved. At one point, some of the tiny branches broke, and he fell to the ground, right in front of me. I was panic stricken. The rake was on the porch, and all I had to defend myself was a set of car keys and my purse. However, the raccoon ran back up the tree and let me leave for work. When I got home that day, he was gone, and I was relieved.

However, the relief was short-lived. A few days later my son was working in the garage, and he came to the house and told me the news.

"You know that raccoon you told me about? I think it's living in the garage. There's stuff knocked all over in there, and I hear something moving above the ceiling."

My heart sank. I was so hoping he had left, and I wouldn't have to deal with him. I went to the garage, into the back where you could look up over the rafters, and there he was, peeking over a board, as if he was saying hello. He was very cute. How could someone kill something so cute, I wondered.

I talked to him and he talked back. Something was amiss here. It was as if the raccoon knew people. When my husband Dann came home, I had him go out and take a look. When Dann began talking, the raccoon became animated, and started walking down the walls.

"Oh, no," I said, "He's going to attack you."

That was the farthest thing from the truth. The raccoon loved my husband, and began following him all over the place. If my husband walked outside, the raccoon walked outside. If he worked on projects in the garage, the raccoon stayed close by. At one point, Dann was working on a car engine, and he looked up to see the raccoon sitting on the opposite fender, looking in the engine like he was helping Dann solve the problem.

It didn't take us too long to decide that someone had hand-raised this raccoon, and for some reason let it go near our house. Why not? We have taken in cats and dogs that people had dropped off, why not a raccoon?

However, knowing the law, I knew I would have to take some action. We couldn't keep this little guy. Also, the neighbors had found out he was here, and they wanted to come over with their guns and do away with him.

I began a phone campaign, calling the local rehabilitators, trying to find one who could take him.

I found out that not all rehabilitators are allowed to take in raccoons. They need a special license. After hours of phone calls, and finding the name of Kathy Britton, I learned she was out of town and would not be back until Monday. I had to wait all weekend to dispose of our new charge. It was upsetting to me for many reasons.

First of all, I was worried one of the neighbors would come over during the day and shoot it. Also, I knew I could not let the dogs out after dark, because they might attack it and kill it.

I had to keep the cats in also, because there was the chance of rabies, and though they had their shots, not all were current, and there were some wild cats in the area who could catch it as well.

Then there was the problem of not being able to go in the house without a fight.

Each time we walked up the sidewalk to come in the back door, Rocky (named by Dann), ran ahead of us, waiting to go in. We'd have to create diversions and run around the house to one of the other doors.

Finally, there was the problem of his food. I had not been feeding him, but I'd guessed he'd been living on cat food, which I leave on high perches in the barn for the barn cats. I took out some cat food and water, leaving it on the garage floor, and I got to witness raccoon eating up close and personal.

First, he'd pick up the cat food pieces in his tiny hands, look it all over, then plunge it in his water dish, washing it fast and furiously like he was washing dishes. Then he'd eat it. It took two seconds to turn a clear bowl of water into a black swamp. Looking up raccoon information on the internet, I learned they liked sweets, so I cut up some apple slices and took them out to him.

By this time, he was back up in the rafters, so I handed him up a slice. He took it in one hand, examined it, and took a bite. It fell to the floor. He squealed, concerned. I handed it up again. Again it fell. Again he squealed. The third time, he grabbed it and sat it on top of the rafter he was sitting on, then he held it down with one hand, and chewed on it happily. This guy was no dummy, I decided.

Aside from worrying about the other animals, we had a great weekend with our new friend. I had told myself he didn't have rabies, he was just too happy, but I still made it a point not to touch him. And we tried to keep him out of sight, feeling the less people who saw him, the better.

Finally Monday came, and I knew I would have to call. I also knew this was Rocky's only chance, because the health department knew we had him, and if Kathy couldn't take him, he would have to be destroyed. We were so attached to him at this point, I knew I couldn't have him killed. I was preparing to travel to another state if I had to, to find him a good home elsewhere.

As soon as I got home from work, I dialed her number. She answered immediately, and I explained the situation. She did not hesitate. "Bring him up," she said happily, "I just got one in and I'm getting four more tonight."

She gave me the instructions for getting to her house, about fifteen miles from mine, and I told her I was on my way.

On Sunday, I'd discovered that Rocky loves Apple Jacks cereal, so I planned to lure him into a cat carrier with a few of those. It worked. He walked right in the carrier. I threw in more cereal, latched it up, and put it in the back of my van. I hopped in the front and we were off.

"Whatever you do, don't touch him," Kathy had warned me. "If you do he'll have to be killed." I was glad I hadn't done that, and that I didn't have to lie about it.

We were down the road about a mile, when he started squealing and pawing at the cage. It took about four seconds more before he managed to open the lock and started running around the van. Here I was, a woman alone on the road with a wild raccoon running around inside her vehicle. I was mortified. Would he attack me, jumping on my head and ripping my face open with his claws?

I pulled into the first driveway and turned around, and we sped back to the house in record time. The entire time I was driving, Rocky was clawing at the windows, trying to get out. At one point, he ran across my shoulders, then he jumped onto the dash board, where he stayed until we got home.

When we turned back onto my road, the children who lived on the corner farm were playing hockey in the road. Who knows what they thought when a crazed woman sped by with a live raccoon staring at them out the front window?

We pulled into the driveway, and I backed into the garage. I opened the hatch and Rocky jumped out, happy as a clam to be back "home." He climbed back up to his rafter, clucking happily, while I stood below, trembling and covered with sweat.

I stood there for a few minutes, then went back into the house to call Kathy. When I explained what had happened, she said she'd be right down. I gave her instructions to my place, and waited for her to arrive.

I went back to the garage where Rocky was still clucking happily, and I put some Apple Jacks into a bowl. He lumbered down the wall and ran over to them, and he began munching away. By this time, my husband had come home from work, and I explained the story to him. We waited for Kathy to arrive, and Rocky scampered around Dann's feet.

When Kathy pulled in with her big van, Rocky ran over to greet her. This was a first. Usually when visitors came he would hide back up in the rafters. It was like he knew she was there to help.

She had on gloves, and started talking to the raccoon. She bent down and started petting his head, and he loved it.

"Yes, he's been hand-raised all right. He is too tame," she said. She opened the van door and pulled out a huge Sky Kennel dog carrier. It was big enough to hold a St. Bernard dog. Inside it had a baby blanket and some cat food. She opened the door and Rocky ran right in. She closed up the door, and I threw in some Apple Jacks. Rocky made himself right at home.

"People don't know what they're doing when they take in wild animals. They keep them till their full grown, then throw them back into the wild, thinking they can fend for themselves, but they can't. If they're lucky, like this guy here, they'll find some kind people to take them in. Most of the time they walk up to some farmer and get shot. Or get killed by dogs or hit by cars," she said.

Although there are many rehabilitators, Kathy is one of the few with the special license needed to care for raccoons. Another rehabilitator in neighboring Orleans County has applied for a grant to be able to take in raccoons there. The price? $50,000.

Raccoons require special caging, and must be kept a long time before they learn to fend for themselves and be released back into the wild. They are fed sardines at first, so they can acquire the taste of fish. Then they are given freshly-caught sunfish, and other fish common to small streams, so they get the idea of what's on the menu other than cat food and Apple Jacks.

The most successful releases are by raccoons that reject the cages, and learn to distrust the people who are caring for them. By the time they are released, they don't ever want to see another human again, as they don't want to be held hostage against their will. Those who enjoy the cages will never be released, and will live with the rehabilitator until they die. Their lifespan is about ten years.

As for Rocky, I made a follow-up call to Kathy two weeks after she took him.

"First of all, Rocky is now Roxanne. She's a little girl," Kathy told me. Then she asked if I'd seen the scar on her stomach. I told her I never got close enough to look.

"Well, whoever had Roxanne first saved her life. She was injured, and they sewed her up. It was a butcher job, the scar is jagged and quite large, but it was enough to keep her alive. I can only guess what happened to her. Either she was hit by a car or ripped open by some other animal, but her first owner saved her," Kathy told me. Little Roxanne had been through a lot.

"She's been vet-checked, had her rabies, distemper and parvo shots, and she is receiving fish oil for her coat," Kathy continued.

"And she doesn't have mange. She was so dirty, her coat was falling out, but she had a bath and is getting skin treatments, so she's coming along well."

Kathy said she takes Roxanne for daily walks, and though she doesn't like the cage, will probably be with Kathy for a long time, if not the rest of her life. She likes people too much.

We were very lucky to find Kathy, as was Roxanne. Most raccoons are not that lucky. The rabies stigma is still the norm in our area, and people are still shooting raccoons whenever they find one. The health department is still arresting people for harboring them without a license, and they are destroying raccoons found kept as pets, even those who have had rabies vaccines. It will take a long time for people to trust again, if ever.

If you find a raccoon, there is always a chance that it could have rabies. Don't touch it, and try to find a rehabilitator who is licensed to take it. If you see one walking around during daylight hours, that is not a sign that it is ill, Kathy advises. "They do like to take walks during the day."

Generally, a sick or rabid raccoon is acting strangely, walking erratically, and will show no fear of people or other animals. But, it will not act like your friend, as our raccoon did, and it will not be playful and cluck to you in voice recognition.

If you find a baby raccoon check with your local police or health department to see what the regulations are in your area. If your area does not allow harboring raccoons, it would be best to have it humanely destroyed than to let it be killed in the wild. Also, as raccoons get older, especially males, they can become irritable and can claw you during mating season, so if you have small children, it could be dangerous to take one in.

Generally, wild life should remain wild. Now and then humans have to step in to save our wild friends when they are in danger. But if you find a nest of healthy animals, whether they be squirrels, raccoons, or rabbits, leave them alone and let nature take its course. It's the best thing to do for yourself and for them.

If you'd like more information on caring for wildlife or becoming a rehabilitator, contact your local health department or representatives from your county's S.P.C.A.

[Editor's Note: After writing the above story, I received a horrific message from a wire-haired terrier owner from Oregon, who was out walking her dogs in a wooded area when they happened upon a raccoon. Being terriers, the dogs tore off after the raccoon, barking and nipping at it, and making it very angry. They were atop a steep cliff, and below was a stream. The raccoon ran down the hill, dogs in pursuit, and all of them jumped in the water. As the dogs began attacking the wet raccoon, it methodically grabbed each one, holding them under with its paws, rolling each one over and over until they were disoriented and confused, and then it drowned them one by one, to the horror and dismay of the owner. Just a word to the wise to keep your dogs on leashes when walking in wildlife areas. You can never be too careful.]

WHEN THINGS GO WRONG: A WARNING TO PET OWNERS ABOUT FREAK ACCIDENTS & THINGS THAT COULD HAPPEN

By Avis Townsend

Sometimes, the slightest mistake can cause an unnecessary death, and heartbreak for pets' families. In case you think you've pet-roofed your house, beware of the following accidents (some have been repeated in the stories above, but we can't be too careful):

Bread wrappers and cereal boxes can be lethal. Dogs, more than cats, love to get the final tidbit from any snack they are eating. One family lost its precious collie when the dog tried grabbing that final Cheerio in the box, and ended up suffocating with the box stuck on its nose. The owners' children found it dead on the floor when they awoke for school. Most recently, a Welch Corgi smothered with his long snout stuck inside a bread wrapper. The owners went away for an hour, left the bread on the counter, and the cat knocked it off, providing a great snack for the Corgi. Again, the owners walked into the house to see their young dog dead on the kitchen floor.

Chicken parts get stuck in the windpipes of small dogs, and without someone to try to pull the meat out of their throats, the dogs will die - sometimes in front of your eyes. It's a helpless feeling.

Ham bones get stuck in rectums. My cousin Jerry thought he was doing his Lab a favor by giving him a ham bone. The dog pulverized the bone, chewing it up in tiny pieces and swallowing it. A few days later, Jerry noticed the dog straining to go to the bathroom. Blood was trickling out, but nothing else. Many X-rays later, the vet told Jerry the bone had gone through the intestinal tract in pieces, but it formed a solid mass as it readied to be expelled and was lodged at the base of the rectum. Fortunately, enemas got it out. Instead of paying $300 for the treatment he received, he could have paid over $1,000 if the dog needed surgery.

Stones and cat litter can blow up a stomach. That clumping cat litter is great for cleaning cat boxes, but if your dog likes to snack on the contents of the litter box, there could be big trouble. If that stuff clumps inside his stomach, it could build up to the point where the stomach could explode. The same with dogs who eat small stones. Eventually, the weight of the stones will burst the stomach, and it's a very painful death.

Cats get blocked: Neutering can cause male cats' systems to form urine crystals, which can block their urethras. If left unattended, they can't urinate. It is a horrible death if left untreated. Symptoms are straining, appearing to be constipated, and peeing outside the box (they associate their litter box with pain so won't go there thinking it won't hurt). In my first experienced with a blocked kitty, I heard this horrific scream in the middle of the night and went running into the hall where my cat was hunched over. I thought his foot was caught in the floor board, the scream was so horrific, but it wasn't, so I knew something was horribly wrong.

I called my vet office and told them he was constipated, straining. They knew immediately it was a urinary blockage. It's a common thing. After going to work at the vets, I knew what to ask. If I got a call that the cat was constipated, straining, I asked if it's a neutered male and when they said yes I knew it was blocked.

Sometimes, just putting a catheter in them and draining the urine, plus treating them with meds does the trick. But many times, the only help is surgery. It cost me $1,200 for the surgery. Vets don't always tell you to get urinary tract cat food when they neuter our boys. They should. Females can get it also, as can unneutered males, but the huge percentage of blocked cats is neutered males.

A blocked cat suffers one of the most painful ailments a cat can suffer. His body is being poisoned by urinary infection. We had one cat at the vets whose bladder did rupture. I don't think he made it.

If you can't afford the surgery, it would be more humane to put him down. He's going to die anyway, so let him go before the agony gets so great he'll go into a coma. We had one owner who couldn't afford the surgery, but wouldn't euthanize the cat. She took him home to die. One of the techs offered to pay for the euthanasia, but she refused, saying a miracle would save him. We felt horrible, wondering how long it took the cat to die. There is no miraculous cure. They will scream in pain until lapsing into a coma, and once their body is filled with poison, they will die. It could go on for days.

Also, in regards to this subject, author Heide Kaminski has a warning to all cat owners. "No one thought of telling me that after I neutered my cats I should put them on a urinary tract maintenance diet. Being a single mom on a very limited income, I bought the least expensive food I could get and mixed it with chicken broth to make it more appealing. Little did I know what could happen, as for a couple of years there were no problems.

"But my two-year-old cat Spice died during surgery for crystals in his urine only three weeks after his one-year-old brother Panther made it through surgery for the very same thing. Crystals are not contagious.

"Both cats got them from the cheap cat food which lacks the elements needed to break down the crystals that form in the urine. I immediately changed cat food, but it was too late for Spice. Everyone who has cats needs to know: DO NOT FEED THEM CHEAP CAT FOOD!!! Especially after the males are neutered, be sure to only buy food labeled 'for urinary tract maintenance.' It may cost more, but it can save you hundreds of dollars for surgeries and priceless amounts of heartaches.

Cocoa Bean Mulch Can Kill: According to the ASPCA, Cocoa beans contain the stimulants caffeine and theobromine. Dogs are highly sensitive to these chemicals, called methylxanthines. In dogs, low doses of methylxanthine can cause mild gastrointestinal upset (vomiting, diarrhea, and/or abdominal pain); higher doses can cause rapid heart rate, muscle tremors, seizures, and death. Eaten by a 50-pound dog, about 2 ounces of cocoa bean mulch may cause gastrointestinal upset; about 4.5 ounces, increased heart rate; about 5.3 ounces, seizures; and over 9 ounces, death. (In contrast, a 50-pound dog can eat up to about 7.5 ounces of milk chocolate without gastrointestinal upset and up to about a pound of milk chocolate without increased heart rate.)

Electrical Cords Can Kill: Both dogs and cats find it interesting to chew on electrical cords, or pull the plugs out of sockets with wet tongues. If they are lucky, they will suffer burns. One of my kitties bit through a cord and her tongue turned green and rotted off before I realized what she'd done. A friend's dog not only was shocked, but the current shot him backward across the room, and his heart stopped. His owner had presence of mind to pound on his chest, and his heart began beating again. But if the owner hadn't been right there, the dog would have been found dead on the floor.

Never Pull a String From an Animal's Butt: So your dog or cat ate a string, and now it's starting to come out, only not all at once, and it's just hanging there, or suspended in feces? **DON'T PULL IT OUT**. Horrible things can result. Their intestines can telescope into each other, causing death if not immediately treated by major surgery involving taking out part of the intestines. And/or, they can suffer a prolapsed rectum, where the actual rectum itself protudes from the animal's behind, also requiring surgery. If you see a string hanging, just take scissors and cut it as it appears, until eventually the entire string will be eliminated with no problem. Remember, the intestines are coiled around inside an animal, and to pull on a string or any foreign body protruding from it's behind could cause those coils to twist, turn, and rupture, all with painful and deadly results. Of course it looks terrible. But wait and watch. If the string or whatever isn't expelled in a day or two, call your vet immediately. Bad things could be happening inside.

Dying pets need to be rid of their suffering. Don't wait for nature to take its course, saying you'll let the dog die peacefully at home. They are suffering, and they don't know why. They can't will their hearts to stop beating, and they don't understand why their beloved master is allowing them to feel so awful. Take them to the vet and let them die with dignity. It doesn't cost a lot of money to have them euthanized. If you can't afford to have them cremated, take them home and bury them in their favorite spot. Keeping them with you a while longer is not showing them love.

For those who grieve: Cornell University's College of Veterinary Medicine has a pet loss support hotline where you can talk to someone about the loss of a pet. The number and details are at: www.web.vet.cornell.edu/public/petloss/index

There is much other information and links to many sites where you can find more help coping with a loss. Many veterinary colleges offer free advice on their websites. Or, you can go into Google (www.google.com) and in the search area type in the problem you are dealing with – for instance, "cat bladder stones." There is a wealth of information on the internet, but you should always check with your own veterinarian if you suspect a problem, as sometimes symptoms can mimic other ailments.

EPILOGUE

AN OPEN LETTER FROM AN EXASPERATED RESCUER

From a rescuer on an Internet Chat Room

[Editor's note: Warning…not nice, and not sympathetic at all to humans]

Dear Mr. and Mrs. Average Idiot,

For those of you wanting to surrender your animal, saying you want it to get a better home, most folks at the rescue houses or shelters have this to say:

1) Do not say that you are "considering finding a good home," or "feel you might be forced to," or "really think it would be better if" you unloaded the poor beast. Ninety-five percent of you already have your minds stone-cold made up that the animal will be out of your life by the weekend or holiday at the latest. Say so. If you don't, I'm going to waste a lot of time giving you common-sense, easy solutions for very fixable problems, and you're going to waste a lot of time coming up with fanciful reasons why the solution couldn't possibly work for you.

For instance, you say the cat claws the furniture, and I tell you about nail-clipping and scratching posts and aversion training, and then you go into a long harangue about how your husband won't let you put a scratching post in the family room, and your ADHD daughter cries if you use a squirt bottle on the cat, and your congenital thumb abnormalities prevent you from using nail scissors and etc., etc. Just say you're getting rid of the cat.

2) Do not waste time trying to convince me how nice and humane you are. Your co-worker recommended that you contact me because I am nice to animals, not because I am nice to people, and I don't like people who "get rid of" their animals. "Get rid of" is my least favorite phrase in any language. I hope someone "gets rid of" you someday.

I am an animal advocate, not a people therapist. After all, you can get counselors, special teachers, doctors, social workers, etc., for your ADHD daughter. Your pet has only me, and people like me, to turn to in his or her need, are overworked, stressed-out, and demoralized. So don't tell me this big long story about how, "We love this dog so much, and we even bought him a special bed that cost $50, and it is just killing us to part with him, but honestly, our maid is just awash in dog hair every time she cleans, and his breath sometimes just reeks of liver, so you can see how hard we've tried, and how dear he is to us, but we really just can't ..."

You are *not* nice, and it is *not* killing you. It is, in all probability, literally killing your dog, but you're going to be just fine once the beast is out of your sight. Don't waste my time trying to make me like you or feel sorry for you in your plight.

3) Do not try to convince me that your pet is exceptional and deserves special treatment. I don't care if you taught him to sit. I don't care if she's a beautiful Persian. I have a waiting list of battered and/or whacked-out animals that really need help, and I have no room to shelter your pet because you decided you no longer have time for your 14-year-old Lab.

Do not send me long messages detailing how Fido just l-o-v-e-s blankies and carries his favorite blankie everywhere, and oh, when he gets all excited and happy, he spins around in circles, isn't that cute? He really is darling, so it wouldn't be any trouble at all for us to find him a good home.

Listen, we can go down to the pound and count the darling, spinning, blankie-loving beasts on death row by the dozens, any day of the week. And, honey, Fido is a six-year-old shepherd-mix weighing 75 pounds. I am not lying when I tell you big, older, mixed-breed, garden-variety dogs are almost always completely unadoptable, and I don't care if they can whistle Dixie or send smoke signals with their blankies.

What you don't realize, though you're trying to lie to me, you're actually telling the truth: Your pet is a special, wonderful, amazing creature. But this mean old world does not care. More importantly, you do not care, and I can't fix that problem. All I can do is grieve for all the exceptional animals who live short, brutal, loveless lives and die without anyone ever recognizing they were indeed very, very special.

4) Finally, for God's sake, and for the animal's sake, tell the truth, and the whole truth. Do you think if you just mumble your cat is, "high-strung," I will say, "Okey-dokey! No problem!" and take it into foster care? No, I will start asking questions and uncover the truth, which is your cat has not used a litter box in the last six months. Do not tell me you "can't" crate your dog. I will ask what happens when you try to crate him, and you will either be forced to tell me the symptoms of full-blown, severe separation anxiety, or else you will resort to lying some more, wasting more time.

    And, if you succeed in placing your pet in a shelter or foster care, do not tell yourself the biggest lie of all: "Those nice people will take him and find him a good home, and everything will be fine." Those nice people will indeed give the animal every possible chance, but if we discover serious health or behavior problems, if we find that your misguided attempts to train or discipline him have driven him over the edge, we will do what you are too immoral and cowardly to do: We will hold the animal in our arms, telling him truthfully he is a good dog or cat, telling him truthfully we are sorry and we love him, while the vet ends his life.

How can we be so heartless as to kill your pet, you ask? Do not ever dare to judge us. At least we tried. At least we stuck with him to the end. At least we never abandoned him to strangers, as you certainly did, didn't you? In short, this little old rescuer/foster momma has reached the point where she would prefer you tell it like it is:

"We picked up a free pet in a parking lot a couple of years ago. Now we don't want it anymore. We're lazier than we thought. We've got no patience either. We're starting to suspect the animal is really smarter than we are, which is giving us self-esteem issues. Clearly, we can't possibly keep it. Plus, it might be getting sick; it's acting kind of funny.

We would like you to take it in eagerly, enthusiastically, and immediately. We hope you'll realize what a deal you're getting and not ask us for a donation to help defray your costs. After all, this is an (almost) pure-bred animal, and we'll send the leftover food along with it. We get it at the discount store, and boy, it's a really good deal.

"We are very irritated you haven't shown pity on us in our great need and picked the animal up already. We thought you people were supposed to be humane! Come and get it today. No, we couldn't possibly bring it to you; the final episode of 'Survivor' is on tonight."

Feel free to copy and send this letter to anyone who needs to read it.

Printed in the United States
42511LVS00003B

9 781933 037387